DALIT TRIBAL INTERFACE
A Ray of Hope for Healing and Restoration

DALIT TRIBAL INTERFACE
A Ray of Hope for Healing and Restoration

Editors

Elizabeth Joy

and

Hrangthan Chhungi

CWM/ISPCK/MWM/NCCI/PCI

2012

DALIT TRIBAL INTERFACE: *A Ray of Hope for Healing and Restoration –* jointly published by the Rev. Dr. Ashish Amos of the Indian Society for Promoting Christian Knowledge (ISPCK), Post Box 1585, 1654, Madarsa Road, Kashmere Gate, Delhi-110006 for Council for World Mission (CWM), London/Meora Worlds Mission (MWM), London/National Council of Churches in India (NCCI), Nagpur/ PCI.

ISBN : 978-81-8465-236-9

Laser typeset by **ISPCK,** Post Box 1585, 1654, Madarsa Road, Kashmere Gate, Delhi-110006.

Tel: 23866322/23
e-mail–ashish@ispck.org.in • ella@ispck.org.in
website-*www.ispck.org.in*

Contents

PART – III
BIBLE STUDIES

PART – IV
ORDERS OF WORHSIP

APPENDICES

Foreword

David J Bosch said, "Mission is a multifaceted ministry, in respect of witness, service, justice, healing, reconciliation, liberation, peace, evangelism, fellowship, church planting, contextualisation, and much more." One cannot agree anymore on this view of mission in the Kandhamal context and many such increasing events in other parts of India.

The realities of violence on the Dalit-Tribal communities in India in general and Orissa in particular are heartrending. I am extremely pleased that this consultation held in Bhubaneswar, Orissa in January 2011 made a historic witness to our solidarity as a national and global community with both the Dalit and Tribal communities in Kandhamal. I hope this will become a model where representatives from all groups especially the ones having the difference of opinion, the oppressive and the oppressed groups can come together to explore the way forward to bring peace, hope and love for all people in every context. This needs to be done by holding on to the values of hope, justice, peace and conviction of transformation as we participate in God's Mission. I believe the coming together of leaders, Scholars. Activists, Church heads and Government officials crossing cultures, denominations, religions and regions has made a forward move to promote Healing and Restoration in Kandhamal and beyond.

I commend Dr Hrangthan Chhungi for the lead role that she took in organising the consultation in January 2011. We do not have all the contributions here (the Dalit-Tribal Communities are still way behind when it comes to put to writing. They are eloquent in speaking and communicating. We thank each one who participated in the panel discussions and other presentations.

I commend this book, 'Dalit-Tribal Interface: A ray of hope for healing and restoration' for the witness it bears and the hope that it brings. I am happy that this book will both bear witness to CWM's solidarity with Dalit-Tribal struggles for justice as well as take us forward with our commitment to its cause. I am sure that Rev Dr Collin Cowan the present General Secretary will journey with the Dalit-Tribal communities struggles for Justice as he has expressed his mind and heart for this cause.

Even as I thank CWM for giving me the opportunity to be part of this consultation, I also wish CWM all the very best in the forthcoming Assembly at American Samoa in June this year, on the theme 'Hope: The language of life' which will come alive only when it touches people like the Dalit-Tribal communities in order to ensure fullness of life for all in Christ.

I hope and pray that this book will be a source and a resource for all who thirst for Justice, peace, hope and transforming mission!

Elizabeth Joy
Participant – MWM
20th April 2012

Introduction

India is a subcontinent that cradles so many rich cultures, traditions, languages, religions, art, architecture, communities, races and ideologies. It exhibits a wide spectrum of cultures from the most ancient times and no other country in the world would have so many languages and cultures as India. India has officially recognized 18 major languages mainly based on the linguistic communities and thousands of dialects. India also exhibits the largest and most number of races mixed within its diverse population – Australoid, Mongoloid, Europoid, Caucasian and Negroid.

India is proud of the Sanskrit language which is more than 5000 years old but is sadly considered as a dead language now. However, many Indian languages are believed to have come out of Sanskrit or shares varied percentage of vocabulary with Sanskrit (considered to have borrowed from Sanskrit). Tamil which is more than 3000 years old is believed to be the oldest living language and it is born in the Indian soil! We are very proud that 58 different languages are taught in the Schools in India. India produces Newspapers in 87 languages, radio programmes in 71 languages and films in 15 languages![1] Will there be any other country in the world to match these highly appreciable phenomena in any part of the world?

India has both given birth to major religions such as Hinduism, Buddhism, Jainism and Sikhism which spread beyond its borders and also provided a very conducive context to accommodate other religions from outside such as Christianity, Islam and Zorastrianism. The deep spirituality of the Indian subcontinent that nurtured multicultural, multireligious and multilingual communities to live with minimal conflicts from time to time but more cordial relationships across has unfortunately become extinct! The religio-cultural, social, political, economic disparities

---

[1] *http://indiansaga.com/languages/*

have destroyed the Indian fabric of mutual love, respect and cordiality spinning off communalism, casteism, racism and sexism. The growth of fundamentalism in every religion adds fuel to the burning issues of communalism. Communalism is used in a derogatory sense here with its negative overtones referring to the negative forces within communities affecting intra and intercommunity relationships.[2]

It is the culture along with other factors like the environment, education, experiences, expectations and employment (CE5 formula) that shapes and molds our critical conscience enabling us to see, judge and act in every stage of our life as we grow.[3] The Dalit-Tribal communities are communities that are socio-economically, geographically and politically deprived communities. As Dr Kaushal points out in her keynote address, Dalits and Tribals are those who were pushed to the exterior in terms of all the above mentioned factors. Dalits were pushed out of the main villages and made 'Untouchables' while Tribals were pushed deep into the forest areas depriving them of the many opportunities to education, employment resulting in exclusion and exploitation.

The present era of Globalisation plays a key role in defining cultures within culture and across cultures. This gives rise to two main tendencies – one moving towards homogenization of cultures and the other creating new cultures within an existing culture in such a rapid manner, visible and traceable within every generation. Both these tendencies are dangerous as people are unable to cope with the speed in which all these occur! Globalisation process has marginalized and alienated the Dalit-Tribal communities even more pushing them out of the market economy making them redundant in many aspects not just a decent employment but every other sphere of life.

India celebrated six decades of independence from the colonial Union Jack, but unfortunately even till today the Dalits and Tribals, the natives of this land are still in the cruel clutches and bondages of caste system looking for a hope of freedom and liberation. Dalits and Tribals are

---

[2] Irudaya, Raj. *Mission to the Marginalised: A Subaltern, Feminist and Interreligious Reading of John 4:1-42*, Asian Trading Corporation, Bangalore: 2007, pp 19ff.

[3] Elizabeth Joy, Lecture on 'Gender sensitization' at Young Women's Leadership Training Programme at National Council of Churches in India, Nagpur in 1999.

aspiring and journeying towards liberation. In their common struggle, both Dalits and Tribals have some convergences and divergences, which are enriching to both the communities.

Particularly in the context of the recent violence in Orissa (the infamous Kandhamal Christian persecution), where conflict in the Kandhamal district flared up between two communities *panos* who are Dalits and *Khands* who are Tribals, that on the surface level came as the issues of religion. With the advent of the outsiders into this land in Kandhamal, *Khand* Tribals have been Hinduised and *Pano* Dalits have been Christianised, and in recent years religion is at the superficial level tools to create and intensify conflicts in this region of Orissa, making the whole series of violence in Orissa appear as religious conflicts. However, a critical analysis of the situation within these two years on the conflict between the Tribal and the Dalit gives us the shocking reality of the deeper socio-economic and political conspiracy against the Tribal and Dalit community of this state and the whole Chhotangapur Plateau region comprising especially of the Central East Zone states such as Chhatishgarh, Orissa, Jharkand, Orissa, northern Andra Pradesh and south-western West Bengal that are rich in mineral deposits like diamond, gold, petroleum, iron-ore, bauxite, aluminium, platinum, etc. This conspiracy has come to light within the context of the whole conspiracy theory propounded by the Multinational Corporations which are hand in glove with the state governments and the Central government in the neo-colonization process. This Conspiracy Theory threatens the very identity and existence of the Tribal and Dalit communities in this Central East Zone in our Indian society today.

Conspiracy Theory[4]

The term "conspiracy theory" may be a neutral descriptor for any legitimate or illegitimate claim of civil, criminal, political or economic conspiracy. To conspire means "to join in a secret agreement to do an unlawful or wrongful act or to use such means to accomplish a lawful end." In the present Indian scenario the classic example of this Conspiracy theory is found in the motif of the Indian Government' 'genocidal policy' against the tribal people especially in the Chhatishgar state in their bid to subdue the Maoist movement.

---

[4] Hrangthan Chhungi "Gender Hegemony from the Perspective of Tribal and Dalit Community" an unpublished paper presentation at the National Seminar organized by Indian School of Ecumenical Theology, ECC, on "Gender Issues Facing the Indian Church and the Society" at ECC during July 13-16, 2010.

Not only in Chhatishgar, this conspiracy theory continues to hound the Tribal and the Dalit community in Orissa, Andra Pradesh, Jharkhand and Bihar. And the Kandhamal infamous riot and killings against the Christian community of the Dalit and Tribal in 2007/2008 was the product of this Conspiracy theory propounded by the Caste-business people. These tribal belt in Chhotanagpur plateau is highly rich in mineral deposits of diamond, gold, petroleum, aluminium, bauxite, iron ore, etc. where the multinational corporations are determined to exploit to the maximum with a close hand in glove with the Government of these states along with the Central Government.

Manifestation of the Globalization with its neo-colonization creates a new master for the oppression and the annihilation of the Tribal and Dalit community in this region. The new master (globalization) interprets the new world order with the new norms where the ruled (the state and central government) are made to believe and affirm the colonizer's ideology, languages and cultures. For a colonized subject to be identified with the master is to be elevated from the old ideology with a hope of liberation from social crises of poverty and disturbances. But more often than not, it turns out to be the colonization of the mind, for it alienates the colonized from socio-cultural, political and religious reality, creating an immense identity crises with pseudo-progress with irreparable social injustice and destruction. A case in point is found in the Maoist/Naxalites movement, the anti-POSCO (the North Korea), Vendanta Aluminium Company (England based), etc.

In this process of globalization, we are facing with a two-tier neo-colonization. The state and the central government are the first victims dancing at the whims of the colonizer and making the Tribal and Dalit community as the second victims in the process creating utmost social and political unrest and oppression. Many are tortured and killed in the encounter, cross encounter and fake encounter, thousands of Tribal people are made homeless and uprooted and evicted from their land, culture and livelihood leaving a whole lot of identity crises for the tribal community in the course of conspiracy in order to make their action in a lawful end. The conspiracy aims at avoiding the consequences of the Scheduled Caste and Scheduled Tribe Atrocities Prevention Act 1989 under Indian Constitution by creating the mass exodus of the Tribal community from their land as the Act Section 3 of sub-section (v) forbids - "wrongfully dispossesses a member of a Scheduled Caste or a Scheduled Tribe from his land or premises or interferes with the enjoyment of his rights over any land, premises or water".

In this two-tier neo-colonization, the women are always at the receiving ends with the most dehumanizing atrocities against them over their dignity of life. Custodial rape, gang rape and torture are common phenomena for the Tribal and Dalit women in this region.

As many NGOs and Civil Society are raising their voice in condemning this kind of hegemonic destructive power, it is therefore imperative for the Indian Church to response to these crises, as being the body of Christ, we no longer afford to remain a silent spectator ...!!

If issues like land, culture, identity, existence, reservation, elimination, inhuman violence against women and trafficking, extinction and religious conversion happen to be the core issues that have been oppressing, humiliating and even dividing the Tribal and Dalit community in the country especially in this region, then these issues need to be addressed on an indigenous table and not only on a religious table per se, which thus far has been dealt that way. In this situation a Dalit-Tribal interface is the need of the hour, so that the many hidden issues behind the religious aspects can be spelt out and addressed in order to educate the society and the church in general and the Dalit and Tribal community in particular for justice and peaceful co-existence. Such an interface will give an opportunity for the Tribal and Dalit community to realize that they are being used and exploited as an instrument to camouflage the socio-cultural, political, economic and religious conspiracy by the multinational corporations, the caste-religious fundamentalists, the state and central government. Both Dalits & Tribals can be partners in building communities of peace, for all that they are concerned is justice and therefore justice matters a lot to these people.

Issues that are mentioned above have been analysed in the context of the Tribal and Dalits oppressive reality in general and the Central East Zone turmoil of our present day situation in particular. The need for the Dalit-Tribal interface has been one of the important agenda of the Council for world Mission from the past few years. CWM had expressed its solidarity with the Dalit-Tribal struggles for justice since 2003 at its Trustee Body meeting in London.[5]

In the wake of the Kandhamal incident of 2008 which increased violence against the Christian community, the commitment made by the participants at the Aizawl regional conference on "Theologising Tribal

---

[5] Refer Appendix 7 in this book and Elizabeth Joy's article on 'CWM's Journey through Mission Education: Solidarity with Dalit -Tribal struggles for justice', pp...

Heritage: A critical relook" in January 2008, mooted the need to meet in Orissa. As a follow up action, PCI promising solidarity and support to Tribal and Dalit communities in their struggles for justice and Liberation, worked with the Mission Education unit to lead this programme as both CWM and PCI felt that this was the need of the hour. Therefore, this International consultation was organized by the Council for World Mission in partnership with the National Council of Churches in India and the Presbyterian Church of India at the Crown Hotel, Bhubaneshwar, Orissa during January 17-22, 2011.

The main Aims & Objectives of this Dalit-Tribal interface were:

1.   To bring together both the Dalit and Tribal Movements for sharing their experiences, listening to each other and inspiring each other.
2.   To draw out the convergences and divergences in their struggles for liberation
3.   To create a common platform and fellowship for Dalits and Tribals in addressing the issues of the day beyond the CWM member churches and Christian organisations in India
4.   To address, who is Jesus Christ to these indigenous people, and how can Dalits & Tribals build communities of peace in their contexts?
5.   To strengthen their network for a united and committed witness crossing religions
6.   To reflect on the gospel from the perspectives of the oppressed and marginalized
7.   To help the church to re-affirm its mission mandate in the light of Dalit and Tribal struggles.
8.   To bring representatives from Civil Society, NGOs, Government officials, inter-faith communities, media and law experts together in order to raise our voices in unity for the justice of the Tribal-Dalit community
9.   To strategise methodologies for liberation with a heterogeneous group from India and CWM Trustee representatives from abroad

The methodology adopted during this interface was basically interfacing both the Dalit and Tribal communities, along with the civil society and the church expressing their concerns. This happened through re-telling the story through eye witnesses. Apart from meaningful Bible studies both from Dalit & Tribal perspectives, there were presentations of analyses of the situations from the media, church leaders, scholars, social and legal rights activists and experts who enabled the participants to understand the causes behind the incident in a deeper level. Meeting with the victims of the 2008 and the series of violence till date (even a few days before this consultation) at Kandhamal was yet another heart rendering experience for all the participants. Though two years had gone, listening to the pain and trauma of the victims brought out the intensity and the depth of violence that was caused in the lives of the Tribal and Dalit communities in Kandhamal. The remains of the damaged houses and church buildings, the surrounding forest where the victims were hiding for their lives speak volumes of the atrocities meted out to the helpless Dalit and Tribal people of Kandhamal. All these activities challenged the church, the social and legal activists to come out from their comfort zones and respond to promote Peace, Justice and Reconciliation for the victims of violence and unjust socio-political, economic and religious structures across India, and with the Kandhamal people in particular.

In this consultation, the local participants were from various walks of life. They were Church leaders, theologians, Civil Society, Government officials, NGOs, Legal experts and social activists, who were basically involved with the re-building and restoration of peace and normalcy in life of the Kandhamal society.

A publication, which was envisaged during the planning of this consultation comes to reality with this book titled "Dalit-Tribal Interface: A ray of hope for healing and restoration", which consists of paper presentations, panel presentations, worship orders, Bible Studies, cultural resources, reflections, statements, including the participants' profile photos depicting the highlights of the consultation etc.

We are very grateful to God that this consultation has begun the dreams of the action plans drawn out during the previous two consultations held in Aizawl in 2008 and Vishakapatnam in 2009. The regional consultation in Aizawl on "Theologizing Tribal Heritage: A Critical Re-Look" that was from 19-22 January 2008 sponsored by the CWM and jointly organised by CWM, the Presbyterian Church of India and the Ecumenical Christian Centre as the Local hosts. This consultation strongly proposed the Dalit-Tribal interface in its action plan. The first follow up programme of this action plan was held in the South Asia Regional Consultation on "Engendering Theology from Dalit-Tribal Perspectives", 10-15 March, 2009 at Vishakhapatnam, India, under the banner of CWM, with the Church of South India as the local host.

Looking at the growing violence that is spreading throughout India, there is a need to continue the follow up of this Tribal-Dalit interface. Therefore a very humble request is placed before CWM and all the other bodies to continue your active role in joining hands with the Dalit-Tribal communities' struggles for justice. As the issue needs to be discussed on a National level, the need is felt for all the churches in India to be represented along with a wider representation from the national ecumenical and non- Governmental organisations.

We take this opportunity to thank each participant and resource person for your contribution at the International consultation in Bhubaneshwar in January 2011. Your participation and interaction goes a long way in history setting a new milestone for Justice to Dalit and Tribal Communities. We hope and pray that you will continue to participate in future through your own networks.

We express our sincere thanks to Rev Dr Desmond van der Water for his engagements with the Dalit Tribal struggles in the last several years. We also thank Rev Dr Collin Cowan the present General Secretary for his journey that he has begun with us. We thank Ella for her cordial and committed services in getting this Book publishes. No words would ever describe the help we received from Fr Niravil George Joy for his continued support in editing. Our sincere thanks to Rev Dr Roger Gaikwad the General Secretary of NCCI and Rev Rama.... for being a pillar of strength at all times.

We hope and pray that this Book will be an eye opener for many who read to understand the intensity and complexity of the issues in the struggles that the Dalits and Tribals face in their everyday lives. We look forward to many of you from varied contexts in India and beyond to join in the struggles of Dalit-Tribal communities in India to realise their dreams of reclaiming their identities and dignity to live as total human beings.

Elizabeth Joy and Hrangthan Chhungi

Part I

PANEL PRESENTATIONS

Dalit – Tribal Interface: Healing and Restoration

Order of Worship – 18/01/2011

Prepared by Rev. Jonathan Leckler and led by Ms.Ennah Nsofu

1. Invocation

Leader: O God of liberation, who have been breaking bondages, leading people to victory and enabling them to overcome the forces of evil, come now into our midst and breathe on us the breath of life. You are our strength and salvation. Come now, O God, to hear our cries. For years, justice has been delayed and denied to us. Come now, O God, to drive away the forces of fear, forces of oppression and shield us with your salvation and strength. Come now, O God, to grant justice to people who cry out unto you day and night.

Response: O God of grace, we acknowledge your presence amidst us, for you accompany those that fight against the cruel practices of caste and several other injustices prevailing in our societies today. Blessed are those who express solidarity with the struggles of Dalits and Tribals, for the Lord strengthens them in times of trouble. The Lord listens to all who cry for judgment.

2. Litany

Leader: In the recent past many people were killed including children and women. Several thousands were displaced in Orissa, especially in the district of Kandhamal, as the religious fundamentalists attacked the Dalits and Tribals. Dalit Pano Christians in Orissa had to bear the brunt of casteism and communalism from both ends, and were trampled under the cruel inhuman attitude of the religious fundamentalism.

Response: O God, you promise to be with us, to deliver us, to protect us, to answer us, to rescue us and to be with us in trouble, where are you? We have lifted up our eyes to the hills, from where does our help come from? Come now, O God of justice, establish your reign, judge the oppressor and rescue the oppressed.

Leader: Dalits and Tribals in India cannot enjoy the religious freedom guaranteed in the constitution of India, for if they choose to convert according to their freedom, they are discriminated against in receiving privileges given by the State ensured to them before conversion into Christianity while converts to other faiths continue to receive benefits. Thus some communities become victims of greater injustice. Their long struggle for justice has been unheard and unaddressed for several years by the governments. Justice delayed is justice denied, and justice denied is justice destroyed.

Response: Who shall loosen the bonds of injustice on us? Who shall undo the thongs of yoke? Who shall let the oppressed go free? Who shall break the yoke of discrimination? Come now, O God of justice, establish your reign, judge the oppressor and rescue the oppressed.

All together: God of peace, we thank you that you have sent your son Jesus, so that we might be reconciled to you in him. Give us the grace to be effective servants of reconciliation within our communities. In this way help us to serve the reconciliation of all the peoples, particularly in Orissa- the place where we need to demolish all walls of separation between people, and unite everyone in the body of Jesus sacrificed. Fill us with love for one another. May our unity serve the reconciliation that you desire for all creation. We pray in the power of the Spirit .Amen

3.   Responsive Reading: A Re-reading of Psalm 140

Leader: When discriminations and violence have taken the foremost part in the hearts of people, and when brutal killings and framing false accusations against Dalits have been on the rise, does not God hear the cries of those people seeking justice?

All: Keep us safe God from the hand of the oppressors, protect us from the violent who devise ways to trip our feet.

Leader: For they devise plan to murder our people and make our future generations slaves to them. They deny the cause of the oppressed and wanted to set forth traps for us. Your people are crying unto you O God, in hopelessness and fear longing for deliverance.

All: You are our God, hear our cry for mercy, you are our strong deliverer, and you are our shield, come down to grant us deliverance.

Leader: *They take the lands, women and make our people stressed. They wanted our plans to succeed, for that they use your people in a more cruel way. We pray and cry unto you* parent God, when will justice be brought to the earth? When will our brothers and sisters get their share of justice?

All: The Lord secures the justice to God's people and upholds the cause of the needy. Surely the righteous will praise God's name and the liberated community will live in your presence.

4.   Confession (Together)

O God of righteousness, we bring our inequities before you. Our relationship with the co-creation has been broken because of our selfishness. We ill-treat our companions in the name of castes and groups, though they are created in your and our image equally. *We bore in our mind the grunt of oppression and our willingness to inflict violence on others . We come to your presence seeking confession for we have tarnished your purpose of creating us. With a repentant heart we come to you, for we have internalized discrimination into every arena of our lives. Many a times, we have been insensitive to the struggles of Dalits and Tribals, we have given deaf ears to the cries of those in oppression and have failed to live up to the values of Christ and his gospel. God we confess for our reluctance to listen to the tears of our Dalit and tribal women and we confess for practicing discrimination within the Churches. Merciful God we have blown away the burning fire of liberation which you have ignited in our minds to do your purpose. We feel dejected and disgraceful to say we have been slaves to the discriminatory practices. Restore in us the Spirit which forces us to fight oppression and seek justice. We ask all this in your abundant mercy. Amen*

5.   Absolution

Leader: Arise; shine for your light has come, the glory of the God rises upon you. Go unto your brothers and sisters to seek forgiveness as the lord forgives you. May God lead us in times of despair and hopelessness and bring compassion to the soul to lighten the lives of the people who are in dark. Let us plant our paths in righteousness, so that the spirit of God dwells among us eternally. Amen.

6.   **Solidarity Song** (*Audio Mode- written by Rev. Raj Bharath Patta, tuned by J. Suzanne Sangi*)

We are the church you are the One we search
We 're on the march, for you are our life's approach
We bear the Cross and overcome our sins reproach
We 're in your reign living the values in perch

Caste or Christ, make a choice now
One gives death and other lets live
To cast out caste, come let us vow
The spirit of our calling lets re-live

Divisions, discriminations and oppressions
Dominations, admonitions and suppressions
O Caste, how cruel are your descriptions
Found within and around our inscriptions

Let justice roll down like a river
Cleansing away injustices forever
Let righteousness flow down to revere
Cleaving up the divisions sever

Come out to celebrate inclusivity
Come back to life burying exclusivity
Cull out to fight darkness in all sincerity
Call out a fast for it's a gain to liberty

7.   **Scripture Readings:** *Matthew 15: 21-28*

8.   **Bible Study:** *Bishop Yuhanon Mor Meletius, Malankara Orthodox Syrian Church*

9. Affirmation of Faith: (Together)

We believe in God, who identifies with those who perform the duty of a care-taker, nurturer, protector and advocate.

We believe in Jesus Christ who takes joy in identifying with the oppressed, who encountered rejection, mockery, contempt and finally emerged victorious over death, because of which we experience hope and new life. We believe in Christ who dies everyday when a women from a lower strata of society is beaten, raped or humiliated. We believe in Christ who raises everyday when we stand for justice, speak out boldly on behalf of the least ones in our society.

We believe in the Holy Spirit of God, the life-giver, comforter, unifier and empowerer in the struggles of the powerless. We believe in one Church, which is called out to serve the needy, where there is no discrimination between people, which facilitates God-human relation with a great sense of fellowship. Amen.

10. The Intercessory Prayers

Leader: Give us, God, a new sense
that justice can be stronger than bribery,
that goodness can defeat greed,
and love cast out fear

All: **Give us Lord**

Leader: Give us, God, open arms
to embrace the excluded,
to protect the abused,
to welcome the unloved,
to reach out to the forgotten, the bypassed, the despised.

All: **Give us Lord**

Leader: Give us, God, transformed minds
to pray honestly for those whom we don't understand,
to find compassion more powerful than pity,
to create the relationships which break through the barriers
to break the bondages of class, tribe, language, caste and culture.

All: Give us Lord

Leader: Give us, God, a meal
at which no one is hungry and all are fed,
at which no one is unwanted, and all are loved,
at which the sick are healed and the broken restored,
at which the grieving are comforted and the lost found.
We pray in the name of Jesus Christ, our Sustainer.

All: Blessed is the one, who touches the untouchable,
who lifts up the poor,
who turns expectations upside down.
no longer rich or poor
no longer higher caste or lower caste
no longer north or south,
no longer spiritual or secular,
no longer empty, but full of your mercy,
Give us your Holy Spirit, so there is no longer any caste,
class or status,
united in lifting up empty hands,,
depending on your grace, in Christ, with Christ, and
through Christ,
all glory is yours, now and forever. Amen.

11.   Pledge of solidarity (*Together*)

We the people of God, pledge in the name of God the origin and the sustainer of liberation that we shall hear the cries of those people in oppression and we shall act on behalf of those struggling for dignity.

We the people of God, pledge in the name of Jesus Christ, the inspiration and strength for liberation, that we shall work to liberate the marginalized who are for many generations pushed into occupations and professions of indignity.

We the people of God pledge in the name of God, the enabler of Justice, that we shall break our silence so that we can come out boldly against the injustices done to the marginalized.

We the people pledge our solidarity with all the people movements who fight for justice, rights and upliftment of Dalits and Tribals with institutions that have taken up the advocacy measures for the defenseless people in the court of law to restore justice.

As we pledge in the name of God today, give us power, strength and ability to remain faithful in the calling to be the channels of transformation, so that we can hear the cries of Dalits and advocate for justice.

12. Lord's Prayer (*Modified*)

All Together
Our God, Creator of the universe, glorified is your mighty name. Let your reign of Justice come to this world, so that Justice prevails when people cry out for self dignity and human-hood. Help us to satisfy the basic needs which we are deprived of. Help us not to transgress even as we are willing to forgive those who transgress against us when they repent. Allow us not into bondage, but set us free from injustice and cruelty. For yours is the cosmos, our life struggles, our empowering and the future. Amen

13. Benediction (*Together*)

May the Courage of Lord Jesus Christ, who is the champion of the oppressed community, the God of justice, who hears the cry of the victims of unjust, and the Consciousness of the Holy Spirit who grants us harmony and peace, stay and uplift us now and forever more. Amen.

A Socio-Psychological Issue before Jesus

BISHOP YUHANON MOR MELETIUS

Bible Study: Matthew 15: 21-28

An Indian author and diplomat Vikas Swarup wrote a novel in 2005 called Q and A. Hollywood director Simon Beaufoy and writer Danny Boyle made a movie out of it. The hero in the novel/ movie Jamal Malik lived in a slum in Juhu, Mumbai. For the Hollywood film makers he was a dog of the slum, so also every one in that situation. Jamal participated in a TV game show and became a millionaire. Still, for the Hollywood film makers he continued to be a slum dog, of course a millionaire slum dog or a slum dog millionaire (I, for now, forget all the humiliating events that happened in the movie for short of relevance. It remains a question whether all Indians are dogs or only those living in slums alone are? Of course it is a movie and it does not take our questions. It gives only the statements of its makers). This is how the rich and the powerful, those who control the world affairs, those who make others slaves for the sake of their own agenda call those who are not equally powerful. Some dogs wag their tail and some others resist. However, many go passive while those who cannot do any of these, but feel the heat go crazy and hysteric. I did not hear many voices objecting the change in the title of the movie.

Matthew 15:21-28. [21] And Jesus went away from there and withdrew to the district of Tyre and Sidon. [22] And behold, a Canaanite woman from that region came out and cried, "Have mercy on me, O Lord, Son of David; my daughter is severely possessed by a demon." [23] But he did not answer her a word. And his disciples came and begged him, saying, "Send her away, for she is crying after us." [24] He answered, "I was sent only to the lost sheep of the house of Israel." [25] But she came and knelt before him, saying, "Lord, help me." [26] And he answered, "It is not fair to take the children's bread and throw it to the dogs." [27] She said, "Yes, Lord, yet even the dogs eat the crumbs that fall from their masters' table." [28] Then Jesus answered her, "O woman, great is your faith! Be it done for you as you desire." And her daughter was healed instantly.

Let me start with a question. Jesus was in the region of Tyre and Sidon, in the land of the Canaanites or Syro-Phoenicians. What business did he have there?

Geographically the western region between Mediterranean and river Jordan where the people of Israel settled is called Canaan (Nb. 35:10-14; Jos. 22: 10-11). This region was populated as early as 3000 B.C. According to Nuzi inscriptions from 15th to 14th C. B.C, Canaan was famous for purple wool from which it got its name. Canaan also may mean 'merchant' (Isa. 23:8). The people of the region were Semitics like the Hebrews. They had independent cities and rulers for each of them. Israelites settled first in hilly areas and then slowly came down to Canaanite cities. From 1992 to 1779 B.C, and again from 1550 till 1225 B.C. the region was under Egyptian rule. Later various groups like Barbarians (from North west),Philistines (from Southwest), Hebrews (from South East) and Arameans (from North East) came and pushed the people of the land to Labanese mountains and Canaanites had to confine themselves to the costal region of Tyre and Sidon which was also called Phoenicia. The Canaanites who were thus pushed to a corner survived by treaty or in subordination (Gen. 9:26; Josh. 17:13; Jg. 1:27-33. There was also social integration and assimilation. Judg.3:1-6).

The Canaanites were engaged in ship building and trade. King Solomon and king Hiram of Tyre (BC 969-936) were friends and cooperated in constructing the temple in Jerusalem and in trade (1 Kgs 5; 9:26-28; 10:11-12). Later Ahab entered in to marriage alliance with them (1 Kgs 16:29-33). Hebrew alphabets and language were influenced by Canaanite language. Hebrew religion also borrowed much from Canaanite religion. But eventually they lost their glory. The attitude of the Jews towards them changed considerably particularly after the exile and return. Jews considered themselves as an exclusive community and everyone else as subordinate and alien. Non-Jews wanted to protest, but were unable due to demographic, economic and political reasons. During Jesus' time Jews enjoyed considerable amount of freedom both religious and social in the region even though Romans were ruling the country. So they were able to continue the dominating and oppressive attitude towards people of the land. They called the Canaanites 'dogs' and accounted them to be much lower in social status.

To sum up, the Canaanites were people of the land and were subjected to invasion, enslavement, oppression and humiliation. Thus, we have in Matthew 15:21 ff., a story of a Dalit woman of Indian sub-continent. I do not want to go to the geographical and historical details in parallel.

I take the story of Matthew than of Mark (7:24-30) which is probably the first and shorter, because Matthew has a longer passage with extended dialogue of Jesus with the woman. The message of the event is given to the Jewish audience of Matthew and hence would speak to our situation as well.

The humiliating tone in the words of Jesus certainly reflects the attitude of the Jewish Christians of the early times and the response of the Church (refer to the situation expressed in the Jerusalem council reported in Acts 15). The primary purpose of the story may not be to present Jesus as a miracle worker since there are several other better stories that will serve the purpose. The whole setting of the story, to me, talks about the social status to which Jesus elevated the woman and her daughter and consequently the whole community of Canaanites. (This can be compared with the story of the Samaritan who helped the traveler on the road from Jerusalem to Jericho. There is a tendency to single out the person who helped the traveler and call him 'the good Samaritan'. I think Jesus was referring to Samaritans as a community, not just one person).

Canaanites or Syro-Phoenicians were a community who faced humiliating treatment and unjust dealing from the Jews who invaded their land centuries back.

I consulted few practicing clinical psychologists to learn a bit about the condition of the daughter of the Syro-Phoenician woman. What is said in the Bible as 'possession' in modern terminology can be called hysteria, the cause of which can be socio-psychological frustration. I think this works very well with the stratified and unjust social order that existed during the time of Jesus.

Since the Canaanites were not in a position to rebel, they took it on themselves. In the illness of the girl, I see an expression of the rebelliousness on her part in response to this unjust social order. The mother is the representative of the older generation of the community that accepted the situation as normal. Her mind was already conditioned and had no problem in being called 'dog' (I have seen this happening in my own backyard in the so called 'god's own country', Kerala). But for the younger generation, it was not at all acceptable. They wanted to change it. But opposition may have come even from their older generation. This would have caused an internal struggle in the mind of the girl which may have affected the person resulting in the form of hysteria. When the woman was taken to the status equal to that of Jesus' own people, the dominant community, the Jews, the girl was 'healed instantly'. Re-establishment of social status provides the girl wholeness.

To achieve this goal, Jesus had to work slowly pushing the woman herself to that end. It was not a one sided act of charity on the part of Jesus. The goal was achieved by the woman herself with the environment and challenge created by Jesus. The woman's urgent need and her love toward her daughter helped her fight for the cause all the way and reach the target.

There is a slow, but steady progress towards the goal. The role of the community around specially that of the disciples is crucial. First, Jesus keeps silence (v. 22). But the woman did not get discouraged and leave. Rather continued to plead and the disciples had to intervene. Then Jesus gets a chance to respond. It is hard to believe that Jesus meant what he said, "I was sent only to the lost sheep of the house of Israel". The immediate question would be, if that was the case, why was he there in the territory of non-Israelites? (Of course scattered Jewish presence was in that region. But was he there just for those few? He had been to gentile territory earlier and had worked miracles there too as according to Mt 8:28 ff). The woman was not ready to accept that reason either; rather she continued to press her case. Jesus' second statement was more humiliating than the first. Jesus further tries to hurt her feelings and calls her indirectly 'dog'. It was not only an insult for her, but also for her own community. With this, while for Jews, she becomes a representative of the community of dogs, but for Jesus of a community that can rise to the status of the Jews or even above them by faith. She challenges Jesus with a valid argument. She does not show any offence for being called a dog. This is a positive attitude on her part. She can not change the way others think of or talk about her. She is concerned of her rights and will go however far to get it protected or granted. Through her valid argument she claims her rights since dogs are part of the family and they too have rights. It is not a question whether she accepts the word others use to call her or not. What matters is what she thinks of herself and her rights. She claims that she too has rights in the family. Those who call her dogs are trapped in their own argument. May be this was an answer of the early Church before the Jews who were so proud and counted everyone else inferior.

Jesus had no other go, but to grant her demand. He gives up and makes a comment on her faith and grants her wish. Jesus in fact was slowly liberating her of her mindset and putting her in the right position. Her urgent need also helped in the process. So far Jesus has been complaining about lack of faith of 'his own' people, the children. Now he was able to appreciate the faith of a person (of the community too), a woman first and on the top of it a Canaanite woman. With this appreciation of Jesus she is placed on the top of his own community. The Canaanite woman from under the table is elevated to the top of it and to the position of the children themselves, if not over them. Jesus had already thrown the children out from the table several times (Mt. 15:14. Take special note of Mt 21:31b. "Assuredly, I say to you that tax collectors and harlots enter the kingdom of God before you").

What happens further is in response to the change of status of the woman and her child. Matthew states, "and her daughter was healed instantly" (15:28). The social upliftment, self-respect reestablished/

restored removes the reason for being angry, rebellious and hysteric too. The girl is thus cured and becomes whole. The new humanity Jesus creates does not validate the claims of children's status or otherwise (gentiles). It only looks for faith that fights all the way up, to be considered equal and established in wholeness (see Peter's address in the Jerusalem Council in Acts 15:6-11. "Now the apostles and elders came together to consider this matter. [7] And when there had been much dispute, Peter rose up and said to them: "Men and brethren, you know that a good while ago God chose among us, that by my mouth the Gentiles should hear the word of the gospel and believe. [8] So God, who knows the heart, acknowledged them by giving them the Holy Spirit, just as *he did* to us, [9] and made no distinction between us and them, purifying their hearts by faith. [10] Now therefore, why do you test God by putting a yoke on the neck of the disciples which neither our fathers nor we were able to bear? [11] But we believe that through the grace of the Lord Jesus Christ we shall be saved in the same manner as they".

We need to put this in perspective!

Let me bring in few questions!!

Why is the Church placed in this world of plurality and where people are hierarchically structured? Is it to protect the interests of the rich and powerful honoring their claims or to plan and workout ways and means of making the weak, the oppressed and marginalized whole? Is it not to recognize, protect, and further help them fight for their rights? Just look at what happened in the territory of Tyre and Sidon and also see Jesus' comment in Mt 11:28 ff (Come to **me**, all **you** who labor and are heavy laden, and I will give you rest. [29] Take **my** yoke upon you and learn from **me**, for I am gentle and lowly in heart, and you will find rest for your souls. [30] For My yoke **is** easy and **my** burden is light").

Why do people call others dogs? People call others dogs not because they are dogs, but because it will help those who call, to work out their agenda easily. First, it will create a subordinate mindset in them and they will always be obedient. They will not demand their rights, rather be content with charity. Second, this will give the oppressors a free ride and will help them continue their oppressive attitude.

The oppressors on the one hand are limiting themselves to a corner and on the other becoming a helpless people. When they realize that they are alienated from others and are a helpless lot, they would try to get help through 'force'. They can do that only until others are submissive to them. Once the enslaved people regain their self respect, the dominant community will become even more worried. So they try all that they can to keep others from claiming their rights. One way of doing it is by demoralizing them through derogative names and titles. This is a universal phenomenon. For example, follow the recent events in the international arena. George Bush complained that Indians started eating more and that is why food price is going up in the US. He complained that more Indians are using vehicles and that is why fuel price is going up. Then comes the movie, 'slum dog millionaire'. Later Barak Obama asks Indians to invest in US. Few days earlier Manmohan Singh asked Indian to eat cheap food items to bring down the food price. Do you get the picture? You save money by buying cheap food and invest that in US so that companies like AIG and others can eat that money up. Our Prime Minister is all for it!

Again political and religious fundamentalists will try to divide people and call one higher and the other lower not because they are so, or because god made them so; but because it will keep them divided and will never be united against the oppressors.

Jesus did not categorize people. He only wanted all to be united in faith. He criticized Jews for not having faith. He hailed the Canaanite woman for having faith. This is an indirect call for Jews to have faith and be hailed by Jesus and the oppressed to gain self respect to consider themselves equal to the oppressor in status or even excel them through faith but never sell them away to the oppressor.

So what shall the Church in this part of the world do? Be present just like Jesus was present in the region of Tyre and Sidon. Work with people to help them slowly move upward and gain confidence in themselves. Adopt a social reformist methodology to emotionally and psychologically liberate them from being oppressed and marginalized. Help them to be aware of their rights and privileges and gather strength to fight for it.

The story of the Canaanite woman with Jesus is a story from our motherland, India (the incredible India, the shining India, the land of the slum dogs). Jesus is here in our midst. An unjust social situation created by humans is prevailing in our country and in our society. Dalits and Tribals, the people of the land are being pushed away from the main stream to the side walk and to gutters to be enslaved and oppressed. Their rights are denied by political, social and religious leadership. People respond to this in multiple ways - some quietly surrender, some rebel violently and some go hysteric. Rather they should see the existential challenge before them just like the Canaanite woman did, and stand together against any kind of denial of their rights and violation of their human self. They have to claim their rights as humans just like any other human being in this world.

Christ should be the source of liberation in all matters with creation and particularly humans. Church representing Christ in this world today needs to act on his behalf. It has two responsibilities - first, to interact with the oppressed to support the correct perspective in the struggle for justice, second, to address the oppressive forces with the power of the word to be transformed. Let us be present and be liberative as our Saviour was.

Healing and Restoration Towards Peace, Justice and Reconciliation of Dalit and Adivasi Communities in India

DR. KAUSHAL PANWAR

I wholeheartedly congratulate the organisers for holding this seminar on such a burning topic at a time when we are witnessing growing conflict, violence and scramble for limited livelihood resources between various marginalised communities all over the country – be it Orissa, Gujrat, Madhya Pradesh, Chhattisgarh and many other such places. I am thankful to organisers for giving me an opportunity to present my views on the topic. In presenting my views, I largely draw upon my own personal experiences of being a Dalit Woman, my interactions with people from various communities, and the nature of casteism, violence, atrocity, discrimination, poverty, inequality and injustice I have witnessed and personally experienced through out my life.

My father was a casual labourer and our family did not have any fixed income. We had to live with the courage to face any circumstances, hard work and the stigma of untouchability. My father's lively smile gave us the courage to bear the hunger and extreme poverty. My father was an illiterate but laborious man who bore the burnt of Zamindari and the caste system. He lived with a pile of loans on his head but never left a penny for us to repay. Today I am proud to say, but for his contribution I would not have been here. Had he not advocated my education in spite of all odds, I could have done nothing. Though my father was illiterate, he insisted and sat beside me while I studied.

I kept on studying and he quietly watched me. May be this satisfied him so much! Everybody in the family was envious about my studies including my mother. May be it was due to her ignorance. Both of my brothers had got married by the time I passed 10th class. Everybody in the family was against my further studies. All what they wanted me was to learn sewing and get married. I confronted many questions which came up as challenges. I wanted to opt for Sanskrit in class 8ʹ and asked the teacher Surender Shashtri for his permission to sit in his class. He dissuaded me and said, "whatever you have learnt is enough for you, you can't handle more. Ultimately you have to work as sweeper in our homes; I will speak to your father". I was determined to take the highest degree in Sanskrit. In spite of all the dissuading and inhibitions, I decided to sit in Surender Shashtri's class. The teacher was furious to see me in his class, "you don't know anything, how dare you sit in my class in spite of my denial? Your father beseeched me to let you study that is why I allowed you this much. You can't be a collector by studying. Ultimately you have to clean our houses". He caught me by my hair and when I murmured that I can do it, he gave me a tight slap on my face. The whole class was stunned by this. I could not understand why the teacher is beating me? Why he did not allow me to study when everybody else was studying, even the girls who were scoring less marks than me? But there was nobody to answer my question!

That day, I learnt a very bitter truth about caste hegemony that whenever people of marginalised community like Dalits and Adivasis (Tribals) will try to break the shackles of injustice, upper caste people will always try to silence you with violence and mayhem. Over time they have very cleverly changed their strategy by pitting one marginalised community against the other and Kandmahal violence is a living example of such a clearly planned strategy.

Now I will come to the issue of healing and restoration with an aim to establish peace, justice and reconciliation between Dalit and Adivasi Communities. There are three parts to my presentation, in which the first part deals with the history of commonality between Dalits and Adivasis all over India to demonstrate that these two communities have been actually sharing a dynamic and cordial relationship; the second part will focus on the communal and hegemonic forces, radical Hindu nationalists in specific and about their designs to 'divide and rule' the Dalits and Adivasis; and the final part will deal with the causes, consequences and what needs to be done by all of us to counter these dangerous trends.

I.   History of Commanality between Dalits and Adivasis

As Historians like Romila Thapar have argued, Dalit and Adivasi community have shared a common history in ancient India. The concept of **Dasa** and **Dasyu** arises from a popular theory that when the Aryan invaders entered into unchartered territory of subcontinent, they faced stiff resistance from the native population for a long period. There were innumerable raids and attacks from both sides to establish control over land mass but due to superior warfare technology assisted by use of metal and vast experience in battle strategies, the Aryans were gradually able to establish their hegemony over the Indian population. The native people who were captured in Aryan raids were later termed as **Dasas** (slaves) whereas people who managed to flee deeper into the forests and engaged themselves in counter-raids were termed as **Dasyus**. Centuries later, these two nomenclatures came to be known as **Dalits** and **Adivasis,** which now remain the focus of communal forces. Gradually, the Aryan conquerers legitimized their action by establishing varna-system and declared the captured natives as Shudra. This fact was acknowledged by Nehru, Tilak, Gandhi, Ambedkar and other intellectuals. Casteism is creation of Brahmins to oppress humanity.

Some Sanskrit literature of Arya Brahmins, that is available today makes mention of some important aspects, related to native population or Mulnivasis. The terminology used for the Mulnivasis is Anarya, Dass, Dasyu, Asur, Rakshas, Ravan and Naga. These were the names given by Aryan invaders to the Mulnivasis. These are not praise-worthy names, but were used to abuse and condemn them. Therefore, it is now proved that these Anarya, Dass, Dasyu, Asura, Rakshas and Danav are the original inhabitants of this country, who, are now referred in the constitution as Scheduled Castes and convert from them to religious minorities.

We observe that the original inhabitants of the land were grouped into three; one, these were the group of people made untouchables and were driven out from the public life and were forced to live a wretched life of animals.

The second section of the Mulnivasis is tribal people, who were forced to live in jungles and hills. Thus we can see that the Scheduled Castes are not Hindus, because they do not observe religious customs of Arya Brahmins. Arya-Brahmins call them Hindus, but have not granted them any rights of Hindus.

Hindu code bill was not applicable to the Scheduled Castes. Thus there is no similarity of conduct, thoughts, faith, belief, customs, religious tradition, language and way of life between Arya-Brahmins and Scheduled Castes / Scheduled Tribes.

The third big section, whom we call, Other Backward Class(OBC) is also Mulnivasis. The are classified as OBC because they have been deprived the right of holding power, acquiring property and possessing weapons (As per manusmruti). When these OBC. group accepted the domination of Arya-Brahmins they granted them religious rights of Hindus, but adopted Puranic system for them, instead of Vedic system. From this, it is proved that this class is not Vedic. We can see that when rights were granted to OBC's as per Mandal Commission, the Arya-Brahmins opposed it most. They tried to hatch a conspiracy against the objectives of the Mandal Commission and were successful in that. From these SCs, STs and OBCs, who are the Mulnivasis have become Sikhs, Buddhists, Christians and Muslims. It means the 95% people of minorities are from this Mulnivasi castes. Arya-Brahmins call them foreigners, especially Muslims. Muslims are not foreigners, but are original inhabitants of this country. Thus we all are Mulnivasis. When freedom struggle of our country was going on, we were dual slaves. The Arya Brahmins were slaves of British people and we, Mulnivasis (original inhabitants) were the slaves of the system established by them, in which we were made slaves, socially, culturally and religiously.

On 15th Aug. 1947, our country India got the freedom, but the people of the country did not get this freedom. Only Arya Brahmins got freedom and we, Mulnivasis are still their slaves. Along with this, another important aspect is that these Mulnivasis were prohibited from taking education, possessing weapons and acquiring property. Because of this, they became helpless, and hopeless and came to depend upon Arya-Brahmins. The Brahmins took advantage of this dependency and made the Mulnivasis, slaves. From the view point based on caste system, it can be seen that the Scheduled Castes, Scheduled Tribes, Other Backward Classes and Minorities are victims of the Brahminical system. Therefore Mahatma Jyotirao Phule, Periyar Ramaswami and Dr. Babasaheb Ambedkar have fixed the objective of their movements to change this social System of inequality.

II.   Communal and Hegemonic forces and their impact

It has now become an established fact that the violence on Dalits all over India is not at all a spontaneous reaction but a well planned operation against marginalized people by the radical Hindu nationalists. Various fact finding reports have clearly observed that the Hindutva forces managed to get people across all castes, classes, ages and even genders to participate in violence, the involvement of the Dalits and Tribals only received particular attention. It came handy for the caste prejudices of people to insinuate that such heinous killings cannot be the act of the cultured Brahmins in the Sangh Pariwar. They alleged that it had to be the barbarous people like Dalits and Tribals to commit such inhuman acts as to rape teenage girls and old women in public, to rip open the uterus of pregnant ladies, extricate the foetus with spike of trishul (trident spear) and stuff the burning rags into her uterus- cavity; throw the kids into bakery ovens etc. It confirmed their mental models hammered out in their minds by their obscurantist socialization and casteist culture that the Dalits were uncultured, barbarous and intrinsically inferior people. It is a fact that the Dalits and Tribals were used in large numbers in violence against Muslims but no one can say that the entire violence was their act. The caste people and that includes backward castes, the torchbearers of the Hindutva, are not to be found in the relief camps because they are not as vulnerable as others who end up there. These people did it and got away with it. Either way, if people are to be charged it always came handy to catch hold of someone like a Dalit. The bias is intrinsic, embedded in the system that readily makes it problematic for the have-nots.

Under the guise of religio-cultural work, the Sangh Pariwar has been working for 'Hindutva' which is essentially a political concept. The religio-cultural concept of 'Hindu' though inimical to the Dalits and Tribals represented, according to many scholars, a dispersed identity that is located in a multicultural and multi-religious tradition and social organization. In contrast 'Hindutva' pretends to be inclusive of the Dalits and Tribals, as the RSS (Rashtriya Swayamsevak Sangh) has declared its opposition to untouchability, (and of course not to castes!) but strives for a monolithic culture and, based on it, a monolithic nation and state as well. The genesis of Hindutva that can be informally traced back to Tilak and formally to Savarkar was based on this political motive to create monolithic and monocultural Hindu rashtra and admittedly it forms the source of inspiration for the entire 'Hindutva' movement – from Mr. Advani's Rath Yatra to the Modi's 'reaction' in Gujarat. It resorted to build a repertoire of cultural resources with intellectual thugs. Hindutva, never hid its fascist fangs right since its birth, and rather showered its praise on the likes of Hitler through its greats like Golwalkar. As for the Dalits, true to their Hindu culture, the Pariwar people first ignored them and then realising their political importance and taking advantage of their frustration, lured them into their fold through their Samarasata Manch or by co-opting Ambedkar as one of their Pratah Smaraniya. They made Adivasi Tribals into Vanavasi, skillfully depriving them of their ownership antecedents and making them uncivilised junglees, Hinduised them through their Vanavasi schools, replacing their Tribal gods with Ganeshas and poisoned them with communal hatred against other religions by organising various campaigns like the "Trishul campaigns" they conducted a few months before the carnage.

Many civil rights people found it difficult to come to terms with how Tribal and Dalit people could unleash violence on each other. Part of the explanation lies in their historical peculiarity, economic crisis, political vaccum, but most of it lies in the motivated manipulation carried out by the Hindutva brigade over a long time. Where the persuasion did not work, the VHP- Bajrang Dal terrorized these weaker sections to show compliance.

III.   Causes, Consequences and our reaponse

Dalits and Adivasis cannot escape the painful realization of being the cannon fodder of the Brahmin- Bania Hindutva forces when the FIRs are filed, their arrests are effected and eventually they are punished for what they have done and even not done. It is certain that the real culprits who conceived and carried out this heinous violence will never be touched. It will largely be Dalits and Tribals who would be made sacrificial goats. Even those who are out of the legal net, the living will be far more stressful in the vicinity of the antagonistic neighborhood. It is said that the VHP/ Bajrang Dal- the violence managers had a meticulous planning in not using the neighborhood people against the victims. It may have helped them in executing their plans but it is not going to help Adivasis or Dalits.

Victims of violence likewise cannot escape a lesson that their traditional retrieving will not save them. Their marginality has so far served only the vested interests of a few among them and shall serve here onwards the agenda of the Sangh Pariwar in identifying as 'they'. They cannot wish away the reality that with mere religious identity they are but a minority in this country. Necessarily they will have to transcend this identity and seek alliance with the forces that are in contradiction, potential or otherwise, with the brute majority. As the present agenda of this brute majority goes, all the religious minorities will have to come together and see common cause with Dalits and Tribals who are the traditional victims of the project that the majority wants to reconstruct. The situation of Dalits and Tribals is largely precarious; backward, divided and disorganized as they are, they could be easily swayed by the Hindutva forces. In fact, a large section of them have already been brainwashed to be in its fold and it would be an uphill task to extricate them back. It is only a demonstrable unity of the anti-Hindutva forces that can win them back. Fortunately, for the proposed anti-Hindutva front there is a sizable section of Dalits whose political consciousness is still in tact. Dalits and Adivasis will have to come forward and embrace them wholeheartedly. Some people, terror-struck by the display of inhumanity in this carnage wished to restore peace between the two communities by educating both the sides on the real precepts of their respective religions. Well meaning though, it betrays the misunderstanding that people indulge in misdoing because of their misunderstanding of religion. It is rather the religion, right or wrong, has been the root cause of people's misdoing. No amount of preaching in the name of religion would bring sanity in people. Let people have their respective religions as their personal faith; let it not come out in the social arena. Let them dust away the traces of religion in the social space so that they can clearly see the relations of exploitation that the system has woven around them. Only the existential concerns, the concern for survival can bring people to senses. Even in empirical terms it is never the religion, but the movements of the toiling sections that eliminate the communal riots. For instance, during the historic textile strike in 1980s, there was no communal strife in Bombay and the influence of Bal Thakre and his Shiv Sena was at an all time low. The surest way to eliminate communal conflict is to subordinate all other identities to the class identity. Beyond the tactics of resisting the advance of Hindutva forces, the strategy of class struggle only could pave way for better tomorrow! Thank you all.

Dr. Kaushal Panwar
Assistant professor, Sanskrit Deptt.
Motilal Nehru College, University of Delhi

CWM's Journey through Mission Education: Solidarity with Dalit -Tribal Struggles for Justice

– ELIZABETH JOY

Introduction

The series of brutal violence and the massacre on the Christian Dalit-Tribal communities in August 2008 and our response to those still facing the brunt of this violence set the backdrop to the consultation in Bhubaneshwar, Orissa, India from 17-22 January 2011. For the very first time representatives from different Indian Churches, and from other faiths, social activists, lawyers, politicians, Government officials, and lay leaders, heads of many Christian and non -Christian organisations came together. It was not easy as we began to take note of what had happened and what is the present scenario and respond to 'what are we called to do at this point of time'? What appeared on the surface to be instigated on the basis of religion and faith seems to go deeper into so many factors. For a clear backdrop and the details of the Dalit-Tribal identities please read the rationale for this Consultation.

How can anyone ever digest the horrible events in August 2008 that killed more than 90 Christians, burnt more than 350 Churches and 6000 homes, rendering 54,000 Christians as refugees in their own places where most of them fled to the forests seeking refuge unwilling to give up their faith? In 2010, there were still 17,000 who had not returned to their villages for the single reason that they do not want to give up their faith in Christ and know that they will be killed for their stand. Even to this day a few thousands are still in the forests, what is our response to these Christians, our brothers and sisters in Christ? As we trace CWM's journey we will definitely arrive at the conclusion that not much has been done, but we have just begun. Can we in the light of our faith, the commitment that we made as CWM – Global communities of Churches in the past, and in the light of our new Assembly Theme under the new structure and the new leadership ensure that we bring 'Hope: The language of Life' in the lives of these people?

Our Solidarity visit to Kandhamal as an eye opener to Faith, Hope and Love in Christ

The series of violence took place instigated by the religious fundamentalists, Government officials and Multinational companies in order to grab their land which is rich in minerals!!! On 20th January 2011, we the participants of the Dalit-Tribal Interface: Healing and Restoration consultation at Bhubaneswar, Orissa went on our Solidarity visit to Kandhamal. It was a very scary journey as we were warned about the Naxalites and other terrorists who can attack us on the high ways. We left early morning by 4.30 am by six cars. I was more concerned about two people – Gwyneth Jones from Wales on account of her skin colour and the Bishop from the Malankara Orthodox Syrian Church on account of the colour of his robe – saffron!!! The former one as a white woman should not become a target of any violence as Orissa has the history of burning foreign missionaries and the place where we go the Christian Dalits and Tribals should not mistake the Bishop for a BJP man (Bharathiya Janatha Party) as this is a Hindu fundamentalist group that creates a lot of havoc and violence on these poor Christian communities. As per my request, Kasta Dip the present Dalit-Tribal Desk co-ordinator in CNI (Church of North India) who was leading the group put the Bishop in our car and Gwyneth in another with safe custodians.

We reached Kandhamal by lunch time and were hosted by the CNI Bishop of Kandhamal Diocese. There we had the opportunity to meet with several people from both the Dalit and Tribal communities. We also visited a few Churches and homes that were destroyed during the violence. The meeting with the family of a lay leader from CNI who was murdered just a few days before our consultation and listening to their agony and fear was heart rending!

One person's story was astounding and filled by being with shock, wonder, amazement and utter submission for the faith and hope he had in God almighty. His name is Junos and aged about 57 years old. His love and gratitude to witness Christ's love in his life never ever decreases. He was one among the many who were tortured by the fundamentalist leaders through the local people. He showed his hands and body which was sprayed with bullets!!! He still has about eleven to be removed as they are very close to his bones and skin. However, he boldly confesses his firm faith in God saying, "Even though that many bullets pierced through my body, not one went through my heart... Isn't this a miracle?... I am alive because Christ is alive!!!" His elder brother died of brutal attacks and his brother's wife became mentally ill after suffering injuries to her skull in these attacks. Junos unlike many other thousands of people who fled to the jungles, refused to do so and also refused to embrace Hinduism which would have spared him from this ordeal. He does not regret a bit for his stand.[1]

This is just one of the persons that we met there whose faith, hope and Love for Christ calls us as Christians from around the World to respond to the plight of Dalits and Tribals in Kandhamal and beyond who are threatened with their lives. They face severe consequences including death if they refuse to reconvert to Hinduism. How can we live out our faith in relation to these communities that are yet to be healed by restoring their identities and human dignity? Many more of these stories are recorded by Anto Akkara who journeyed with us to Kandhamal. His book titled 'Shining Faith in kandhamal' narrates many stories that would rend our hearts as we see the pain, torture and massacre that had taken place in Kandhamal but it also deepens our hope in God and instils in us the urge to translate our faith in action by reaching out.

---

[1] Akkara, Anto. *Shining Faith in Kandhamal*, Bangalore: Asian Trading Corporation, 2010, pp. 49-51.

Tracing CWM's Journey in relation to its commitment and response to Dalit-Tribal struggles for justice

The purpose of this paper is to briefly articulate CWM's role in the life and struggles of the Dalit-Tribal communities especially in the Indian Sub-Continent. An attempt towards tracing this role begins with recapturing the passion and compassion that moved CWM to act in the past. This is followed by mapping the actions during the period 2002-2011 that witnesses to translating CWM's faith into action through its engagements in Dalit-Tribal liberation struggles. Finally, our commitment to building transforming communities of hope and love by translating our faith into action is visualised on the basis of the shifts in our mission engagements for the future.

CWM was born as an experimental body in 1977 in Singapore. Although it existed as Congregational Council for World Mission (CCWM) from 1966 which was a significant move from London Missionary Society (LMS) that existed from 1764-1966 and Commonwealth Missionary Society (CMS) which existed from 1836-1966, CWM from its inception committed itself to be a Global Community of Churches to be engaged in one world mission. The main focus was to facilitate mission by equipping the member churches. Two main recognitions or affirmations that shaped CWM as a unique Mission organisation were the emphasis on its commitment to mutually share resources (every church becoming a receiver of help and a sharer of its talents and resources) and change the direction of Missionaries sent from unidirectional to multidirectional mode.

The first affirmation expressed a strong commitment made to share its resources such as finance, people, skills and insights globally to carry out the mission locally. This enabled every member Church however big or small however rich or poor to believe, contribute and receive, bearing witness to its founding statement formulated in 1975 saying, "No particular church has a private supply of truth or wisdom or Missionary skills".[2] One of the founding principles was also mutual sharing well expressed by the following statement: "We believe we

---

[2] *Sharing in one world Mission*, Council for World Mission, London: 1975..., P3.

become participants in Mission not because we hold all the truth, but because we are part of the body of Christ. All of us are searchers".[3] The second affirmation was the humility to accept God's gift bestowed on every Church however small or poor. This pointed to the shift from the Missionaries going from North to South or West to East. Thus the movement of Missionaries from, 'Everywhere to Everywhere' was practised enriching all its 31 member Churches to experience the enriching quality and witness in such a diverse Missionary engagement. This new structure brought the 31 member churches around the table giving them an equal voice to come together and decide as to how they will use their resources. This makes CWM a very unique and special Mission organisation even to this day.

This paper specifically aims to focus on Mission Education unit and its contribution to the Dalit-Tribal struggles for justice. As we look back at the history of CWM, the role of Mission Education has been central to the work of CWM since the formation of CWM in 1977. Over the years, Mission Education has functioned under a range of identities such as Education Department, Education in Mission unit, Mission Development and Education unit, and Training in Education unit! Despite this frequent change in its name, the unit's vision has promoted an effective mission in CWM's overall history. It was initially headed by the General Secretaries where Rev Bernard Thorogood and Rev Dr Christopher Duraisingh have given their able leadership. Rev Dr Roderick Hewitt headed this unit as the Secretary for Education in Mission and also contributed much to this unit as the first Moderator of CWM in its new venture with a new structure from 2003-2009. Rev Dr Prince Dibeela the present Moderator has also showed keen interest and conviction in participating in the struggles of Dalit-Tribal communities even prior to him taking up this role. As the Principal of the Theological College in Botswana, he attended the Global Theological Education Consultation organised by CWM in 2003. He was a passionate listener and one who believed in overcoming all these oppressive structures to make people from the margins move to the mainstream to become visible.

---

[3] *Ibid.*

Ms Francis Brienen as the Associate Secretary headed the Mission Development and Education unit as well as the Training in Education unit from 1991until 2001 when the Council decided to change it finally to Mission Education unit. I, Elizabeth Joy was appointed as the Executive Secretary for Mission Education. I am indeed very grateful to God for enabling me to be in God's Mission in this capacity from October 2002 until January 2011. I am also proud that I could work for almost the entire period with Rev Dr Desmond Van der Water as the general Secretary. If not for his encouragement and support, what CWM has achieved hitherto would not have been possible in relation to CWM's solidarity with Dalit-Tribal struggles for justice. I was equally privileged though it was for a very brief period to work with Rev Dr Collin Cowan as the new General Secretary (just the last one month). I see a deep commitment in him to support the Dalit-Tribal struggles for justice. I am sure that as he takes on the baton from all of us who have completed our role as staff of CWM, he would take CWM to higher levels of mission to bring fullness of Life in Christ for all. I believe in his faith convictions and promises to keep this on CWM's Mission agenda to support and journey with the Dalit-Tribal communities even within the new structure.

Our Love and compassion for Dalit struggles: When and where did we begin?

Encountering Dalit issues

Three of the CWM member Churches from India – The Church of North India (CNI), the Church of South India (CSI) and the Presbyterian Church of India (PCI) as well as the Church of Bangladesh (COB) from the South Asia region comprise of Dalit/Tribal communities or both. The struggles of Dalits and Tribals go far back in history where they have been expressing their oppressed, dominated and dehumanised contexts at different levels within their socio-political and economic structures. However, it has taken much a longer time for these communities to express their yearning to be affirmed as humans beings created equally in God's image as any other person belonging to any other caste, class, race or colour.

It is indeed a very painful process first of all to accept the imposed subservient identity. It is much more daring and vulnerable to resist this imposed identity as 'Untouchables', out castes, identities with all the shame, deprivations and pain that it has brought and can bring even more with such a daring move. Therefore, as we see the history of CWM where we specifically look at its role from 1977, we would not be able to trace anything distinct in its early historical period. Indeed, one can never underestimate the role that Missionaries in General as well as London Missionaries in particular have played contributing to the empowerment of Dalits and Tribals through the education that was made available for them. If not for their missionary work and intervention, the Dalit-Tribal communities would not have had an access to Education. Education brought with it the empowerment both in terms of employment as well as understanding the Christian faith that enables these people to believe that they do not deserve such inhuman treatment for any reason. It is this conviction that instigated and motivated them to question the oppressive structures that stood firm for more than 3000 years! This structure divided the people and stratified them into different castes imposing worst forms of slavery, racism, gender discrimination, and considering a section of the people as 'Untouchables' segregating them based on the concept of 'purity and pollution'.

The word 'Dalit' is a Sanskrit term and the root 'Dal' in Sanskrit and Hebrew means broken, crushed, destroyed, split, rent asunder, exploited, oppressed etc. This term 'Dalit' was coined by Jyotirbai Phule, a great social reformer in the 19th Century.[4] Dalits are people who believe that they have been dehumanised based on the concept of Purity and pollution and act to get rid of this polluting identity. For generations they believed, accepted and internalised this notion that they are polluted and polluting people. Dalit is the name that they have chosen for themselves to describe their situation and their status.

So, the changes that took place in the social context soon affected the Theological landscape of India. Understanding Casteism as an evil structure, slowly and steadily enters the life and witness of CWM. Thus we need to note that although MS Daisy Gopal-Rathnam from

---

[4] For details refer James Massey, "Historical Roots" in James Massey (ed). *Indigenous People:Dalits,* Delhi: ISPCK, 1994, PP4-6

the CSI was the first chairperson of the new CWM in 1977, and Rev Dr Christopher Duraisingh was the General Secretary from 1985-89, one would not find the term Dalit or Dalit programmes until 1995-96. It was in the early 70's that Dalit Theology was articulated and slowly in the making. It was not very well received or accepted in the initial stages. There were so many issues of stigma and pain even to talk about it or for a person to say that he or she belonged to the outcastes or the Untouchable communities. It took more than 10-15 years for people to grapple with it, affirm it and take courage to articulate with their painful experiences as well as Faith convictions. Therefore, Dalit issues were brought to CWM's notice much later in the 90's only, initially through the Training in Mission (TIM) programme of CWM.

Training in Mission and Dalit Issues/Dalit Theology

Training in Mission or popularly known as the TIM programme is the most popular among all programmes or training events in CWM. It began in 1981 within four years after CWM was formed. It was right from the beginning except for a year in 2002 (just before I could join) developed, designed and co-ordinated by the Mission Education unit under its varied names. Initially, when this TIM programme began, it was held in UK and Jamaica for five months each. The Jamaica leg was moved to Tamilnadu Theological Seminary (TTS) in India and then the UK leg to South Africa in 1995 and 2000 respectively.

It was Ms Francis Brienen, the Associate Secretary of Training and Education unit who worked on the relocation of the TIM leg from Jamaica to India. It was she who along with Madeline Logan the senior Programme secretary of this unit who did everything in relation to choosing the next venue for TIM. I would like to sincerely extend my thanks and very deep gratitude to her for her visions and goals in choosing the Indian Context and more specifically the TTS. I am also very grateful to Rev Dr Dhyanchand Carr the former principal of TTS who worked with Francis to provide a very conducive environment for TIM to continue in India. It was indeed my pleasure and honour to work with the Indian Co-ordinators Rev Paul Reginald and Rev Dr Samuel Soundarapandian from CSI. It was my pleasure, privilege and honour to work with the Indian co-ordinators Rev Dr Dorairaj, Rev Nancy Singaram, Rev Dr Kerstin Naumann, Rev Maggi Larbeer, and

Rev Dr John Samuelraj. They as well as the entire TTS staff and students have contributed much to each TIM candidate's life and witness since 1995 for 15 years. They along with the excellent support from the other two Principals Rev Dr Mohan Larbeer and Rev Dr Gnanavaram made it possible for more than a 150 TIM Students to pass through this 'Life Changing' Programme as it is mentioned by almost all of them!

TTS being an innovative place where the students are trained to do Theology in very practical and challenging situations to bring out the best in them, has proved to be the best place for TIM programme. The students who have passed through the portals of this great Institution would bear living witness to how this entire community has shaped them, formed them and challenged them to believe in a God who acts in history beyond all discriminations and barriers. They would testify to the manner in which their faith was challenged and re-established with firm faith convictions in God who liberates people from all bondages in relation to caste, class, gender, religion and faith to bring about liberation and justice at every level of oppression especially for the Dalit people. Every TIM student who has been a part of this community has taken home the essence of Dalit Theology and the struggles of Dalits for justice. I even heard that it was one of TIM candidates who challenged the former GS of CSI to bring this issue to the forefront in CWM to be on its Mission Agenda!!! We have young missionaries who are around the world standing up in solidarity with the Dalit struggles for liberation, identity and dignity.

I have ensured that every TIM student from 2003 -2010 batch have understood the Dalit Struggles for justice and the essence of Dalit Theology even when they are in South Africa – their first leg of TIM during the orientation period itself, (within the first two weeks of their arrival), so that they are aware of it when they come to India to see it in reality and explore with the TTS community the issues related to Dalits in detail. I have taken special sessions on Dalit issues and Dalit Theology, introducing it to them so that they reflect on it even as they learn about racism to compare and realise the depth of pain for people who bear the brunt of these issues.

Exploring mission in relation to Dalit-Tribal contexts

The Inaugural Assembly of CWM at Ayr, Glasgow in 2003

The Inaugural Assembly of the new CWM Structure took place in Ayr, Glasgow, hosted by the European region. It was hardly eight months since I had joined CWM. We the staff went to Ayr on 10th June to attend the Assembly and the Trustee Body meeting. We went a few days in advance as this was the first of its kind bringing so many delegates from around the world. The delegates had an exposure programme to different churches and their Mission Projects during the weekend (20th -22nd June). We the staff were to stay back and do some preparatory work for the rest of the event.

Rev Micheal Heaney, the General Secretary of the Congregational Federation (CF) in UK, who was then the Chair of Corporation for CWM, had invited me to go to one of his Churches for the weekend exposure to be a resource person and to preach in a Church in Nottingham on Sunday. My General Secretary permitted me to go and I as the CWM Executive Secretary for Mission Education decided to speak on Dalit people and issues of caste system in India both at the workshop as well as during the message at the Church in order to address the theme of the Assembly, "Who is my neighbour?" That was the first time I raised the struggles of Dalits for justice and our response and solidarity in a forum in CWM other than TIM. Ever since then, I continued to raise my voice against caste discriminations and its impact in destroying communities.

CWM Global Theological Consultation in 2003

The CWM Global Theological consultation was held in Johannesburg from 29th Oct – 4th Nov 2003 on the theme, **"Transforming Theological Education"**. This consultation brought together many Theological Scholars from around the world especially the CWM member Churches. The CWM Executive Secretaries of the programme units – Rev Dr Jooseop Keum from the Mission Programme unit, Elizabeth Joy from Mission Education unit and Rev Dr Andrew Williams (the one who gave the lead) from the Personnel and Training unit came together with the General Secretary Rev Dr Desmond van der Water to organise this consultation along with a global working committee.

Having explored the different contexts – African, Caribbean, East Asian, European, South Asian and the Pacific, it became very clear that there could be 'no global understanding without the local'. It was agreed that if CWM wishes to increase its commitment to Mission, it needs to raise its Mission profile. It was clearly noted that the Mission profile cannot be raised just by adding Mission studies to Theological Education but the entire Theological Education needs to be re-looked.

It was once again affirmed that in the back drop of the global reality, the whole world enters our home. Gobalisation is the key word in Economics, Politics and culturisation. Theological education and constructing local theologies had to come to grips with this factor. This once again brought into focus the issue of communities that are being more and more marginalised and the need for constructing Theologies and responding to theological Education itself to come not from the four walls of the Colleges/Institutions but the realities of the worshipping communities/churches.

It is very clear that in doing Theology, we are enabled to do our ministries effectively. The Indian Theological Scholars raised their voices in one accord to bring home the point that it is not the monopoly of the few elites but those at the margins as well as the local realities to form the key resources for local Theologies such as the Dalit Theology. It was also affirmed that Theological education has to take people into consideration. In the Indian situation, naturally Dalits and Tribals had to be given a prime place and their lived realities be taken into consideration to make the Indian Christian Theology meaningful to majority if its people's experiences. The need for the Gospel to be inculturated in its context was upheld. The patriarchal, caste, class and race dominations within Theological Education and the dominant Theologies were seen as areas where changes had to be brought in to make it more relevant for the communities struggling to find their identities.

The Indian participants especially from the Church of South India and the Tamilnadu Theological Seminary (Rt Rev Dr Devasahayam and Rev Dr Isaac Kadirvelu) voiced their views that CWM give heed to the cry of Dalits from the Indian sub-continent and address the issues of caste within the Church. Elizabeth Joy led one of the workshops using the Narrative Quilts that each church delegation was asked to bring to share the stories from their context to throw more light on local Theologies and Theological Education. The Indian group presented their narrative Quilt on Caste issues and Dalit Theology. This same group also equipped the then General Secretary of CSI, Dr Pauline Sathyamurthy to be their spokesperson in the following CWM Trustee Body meeting held in London.

Dalit-Tribal struggles for Justice getting a high priority status in CWM Mission Agenda

Dr Pauline Sathyamurthy's story of the 'Mathamma' children who are abused sexually in the name of God and religion (by dedicating them to Goddesses which is called the 'devadasi' system), made the entire trustee body speechless and shocked. Therefore, a small committee was constituted with Elizabeth Joy the Executive Secretary for Mission Education to bring a brief rationale on the Dalit Issues and HIV & AIDS issue to the Trustee Body the next day (1st December 2003) for CWM to address these issues at global level.

Having worked with the Student Christian Movement of India in different capacities, as the former General Secretary, Women's desk Co-ordinator I had visited various tribal regions in India and seen their plight as well as their struggles for justice. The sharing of the Indian realities in relation to prevailing caste discriminations and its impact on the Indian Church, its Theology, its Worship and witness brought Dalit issue to the forefront of CWM's Mission agenda. The Tribal communities also have been bearing the brunt of exclusion and denial of justice, identity and dignity though it may not be as dehumanising as the plight of Dalits. Since I had the passion for their liberation also and felt that until Dalits and Tribals come together and demand their rights to experience the total Human liberation, it will be a distant vision and goal for both groups. They cannot fight separately on their own especially in contexts where they lived side by side as in Orissa. As we can see the Indian History, the communities that were driven into the forests by the Aryans are the Tibals whereas the communities that were over-powered and kept outside their villages as non- humans are the Dalits. They had join hands and fight for their rights and human dignity. Therefore, even though this small group was asked to focus on Dalits, their struggles and quest for liberation, I explained it to the small committee the need to combine and bring these two groups together. It was well received and I took the lead to write down a rationale for CWM to lift up Dalit-Tribal struggles for Liberation as a priority Mission Task for CWM on a global level. So the group worked on it and presented it to the Trustee Body (TB). The entire body with a strong support from the then Moderator Rev Dr Roderick Hewitt, upheld it as one of the three Priorities in the Mission Agenda of CWM, the others being HIV & AIDS as well as Mission with Children. I was asked to present a position paper on Mission with Children (MWC) at the next annual TBM in 2004 at Durban, South Africa which enabled MWC to take off. The TB made clear resolutions for CWM to work with these communities and organise programmes with them to express our solidarity and explore ways and means to bring healing, restoration and wholeness, in ways CWM could express its solidarity.[5]

The following decision was taken at the TBM held in London in 2003:

"Therefore, taking into consideration the magnitude and the urgency of these issues and the grave situations which are an affront to human dignity, respect and the right to life, it is recommended that the two working groups be assigned with the above responsibilities. The working groups shall be constituted with one member from each of the constituent churches, and shall determine their own modus operandi but in consultation with the CWM General Secretary. The Trustee Body agrees in principle that in the event of financial resources needed for the working groups activities to achieve the above tasks, the CWM Moderator, Treasurer and General Secretary shall be consulted."[6]

---

[5] The rationale and CWM TB decisions: The Oppressed Communities (Dalit and Tribal Struggles) and CWM Solidarity towards their Liberation written by Elizabeth Joy, was presented by the small committee consisting of Rev Dr Desmond van der Water, Rev Dr Pauline Sathyamurthy, Rev Dr Lala Rasendrahasina and Elizabeth Joy on 1st December 2003.

[6] Refer Appendix 7 in this book for the Rationale presented to TB in 2003.

The Rationale presented to the TB in 2003 gives a detailed information about the reality of Dalit-Tribal communities.

Follow up action from CWM

The above decision was taken up in relation to HIV & AIDS as well as Dalit-Tribal Struggles for liberation. Both programmes were put under the General Secretary. He requested the Executive Secretaries of Mission Education and Mission Programme to choose one of the above. Since I had a passion to address the HIV & AIDS issue, and thought that I could address Dalit-Tribal issues even from HIV & AIDS as well as Gender and MWC programmes, I chose HIV & AIDS and began working and networked with other organisations at the global Ecumenical level. I am also proud to report that through Mission Education unit, I worked with a small group of members and brought out the CWM Policy and the Strategic Guidelines document which was adopted by the TB at its meeting in New Delhi, India in June 2005.

The Executive Secretary for Mission Programme was assigned the CWM Solidarity with Dalit-Tribal Struggles for Justice programme. He worked at depth with Mr Stanley from Orissa and others. Unfortunately, there was not enough support for the General Secretary and the Executive Secretary from the member Churches to take it forward as a priority at the member Church level.

The Mission Education unit could not succeed to get exposure visits for Team visits programme in CNI even after repeated requests in 2004. With much pressure from the CWM secretariat staff, CNI arranged a very meaningful exposure visit for the TB in 2005 at Delhi. The TB was taken to a rural Church and Rev Fr Monodeep Daniel who is the head of the Brotherhood of Ascended Christ, Delhi gave an excellent presentation on the crux of this Caste issue. He explained why the Church hesitates to carry forward its mission to the Dalits explaining the Stigma and its impact on people who have taken lots of trouble to get over or hide that identity. Even though the problem is not solved at a deeper level, it is a very sensitive issue but definitely needs to be addressed.

Initially CNI was reluctant to accept that the Dalit-Tribal issue was their issue. However, with the efforts which Rev Dr Enos Das Pradhan and Sudipta Singh took at their Church level, they announced in 2007 at the global Partners meeting at Srinagar, Kashmir that they have identified the Solidarity of the Church with Dalit-Tribal communities as the priority and it appeared on top of their Mission Agenda!!! Soon CNI established a desk also and now a full time person is appointed as the co-ordinator. Kasta Dip the former Youth co-ordinator of CNI is the first person to take up this position. I extend my heartfelt thanks and deep appreciation to the CNI and its leaders who could respond so positively at a short span of time. So it was not an easy process even for the leaders in CNI to walk their talk and be faithful to God in ensuring solidarity with these communities.

In 2008, when the spate of violence broke out in Kandhamal in August, CNI was found immediately in the scene through its constituency there. In their 13th Synod Assembly held in October 2008 in Pattankot, Punjab, CNI had special sessions on addressing Kandhamal issue and we heard from people who had experienced the horror of violence with physical and mental injuries narrating their painful stories. I still vividly remember the interview Rev Dr Enos Das Pradhan had with the media and his courageous stand for the Dalit Christians in Kandhamal openly and publicly. It is not easy to do that especially being in that disturbed context which was very risky indeed. I am indeed so very proud of him for the stand he took and the manner in which he responded to this violence voicing out the Church's witness very boldly. Sudipta Singh as the Programme co-ordinator of CNI as well as the South Asia region of CWM had exhibited a gallery of photos in addition to bringing people with the help of the local leaders. It took people a lot of courage even to look at those photos depicting the most cruel and heinous acts of violence on the Dalit Christians in Kandhamal. So CNI's journey and contributions at this period in the life of Kandhamal is note recording with a sense of gratitude and pride.

In CSI, due to internal problems even those who raised their voices so loudly for CWM to intervene to combat Dalit –Tribal issues related to exploitation, exclusion and alienation could not come together even when the General Secretary and the Executive Secretary for Mission programme tried their level best between the years 2003-2007.

However, CSI already had its Dalit Desk since a long time. In 2009, CSI provided very challenging exposure visits to the delegates of the CWM Assembly as we focussed on the theme, 'Live the Good News'. Therefore it had to be left unattended for a longer period until as the latter left CWM to join WCC.

In 2009, the other exposure which created a lot of heat and dust especially among the youth and the Participants from American Samoa was the Gender discrimination with respect to the trans-sexuals. CSI is doing a commendable work but there is so much that they and other member Churches can learn from American Samoa and Samoa where you see how these communities uphold include the trans-sexuals as part and parcel of the families. They have no difficulty in being accepted or being employed contrary to the very oppressive response from within the Indian Contexts. After the exposure visits to these community members (Trans-sexuals), the delegates from American Samoa – Meora and Mrs Elia Taase were very keen to have a team visit from CSI to their country for an exposure to the way the trans-sexuals are accepted within the Church and Society. I was pleasantly surprised to hear and see that they were part and parcel of everything in the Church and community unlike in India and many other countries. Even though we worked closely with the GS of CSI and these two members from American Samoa, we could not organise the Team visits due to the Tsunami that struck the Samoan Islands in 2009. It took time for them to recover from their situations after this Tsunami and I left without fulfilling this dream of mine. I am sure that the coming Assembly would be one of the best spaces for the CWM member Churches especially from CSI and CNI to have their exposure visits. It would be worth taking a few Trans-sexual persons from the group that we met during the Assembly or any members with whom the CSI works currently with. I am sure CWM can boldly be a 'Hope: the language of life' even as you begin to explore this dynamic theme by being practically engaged in such acts as these to bring the marginalised communities to the mainstream.

In 2007, PCI had approached CWM for an ecumenical grant for a joint consultation with the Indian School of Ecumenical Theology (ISET) at the Ecumenical Christian Centre (ECC) on the theme, "Theologising

Tribal Heritage: A critical Re-look. Since the application was not given with the required time notice, it was not possible to consider it positively. However, Rev Randolph Turner inspired and asked if they can be requested to postpone this event so that it can be considered positively as it is important. I had actually declared conflict of interest as Dr Hrangthan Chhungi from IEST was my sister-in-law and therefore did not add my views to the discussion. When repeatedly pressed for my comments on that event, I reminded them that we had actually lifted up the Dalit-Tribal Struggles for justice as our priority Mission Agenda. Therefore, it will be worth exploring if PCI and ISET are ready to widen it up as a regional event including Church of Bangladesh, CNI and CSI. Then we could participate at a regional level fulfilling the mandate given to secretariat staff by the TB. PCI as well as ISET were more than willing to postpone as well as have it as a regional consultation. It was indeed Dr Des van der Water who insisted that I journey with this programme and address the Dalit-Tribal struggles for justice. Therefore, it was with a special request from the General Secretary I took up this programme and also followed it up with two more events before I completed my contract with CWM.

In 2007, when CWM celebrated its 30th anniversary in Singapore with the theme, 'Partners in Mission: the practice and the promise', it addressed the Dalit-Tribal issues of identity and dignity under the marginalised and oppressed groups.

Mission Education unit on behalf of CWM also organised jointly along with WCC and WARC an international Ecumenical conference in commemoration of the 200th Anniversary of the abolition of the British trans-Atlantic slave trade act. This conference was held in Jamaica from 10-15 December 2007 and Rev Dr Collin as the GS of UCJCI then was the host. We teased out the issues in all communities in the margins. The similarity between Caste and racism was well acknowledged.

The regional consultation held at Aizawl at the end of January 2008 was very successful. Since in Orissa the Dalit-Tribal communities had just experienced a series of violence, it produced a lot of heat and dust, passion and commitment for the cause of Dalit-Tribal justice and Liberation. A deep commitment was expressed for the Tribal communities beyond North -East India. Since the Bishop from CNI and Lutheran Churches in Orissa were there, they shared their agony and pain due to all the assaults and violence. Solidarity was expressed. The report, statement and recommendations for future action plan were clearly spelt out.[7]

Apart from the above mentioned events, Mission Education unit addressed the issues of Dalit-Tribal at the Global Youth Convention held at Johannesburg from 15th -22nd June 2004. Through Team visits it had enabled representatives from different Churches to have a first-hand experience of what Caste discrimination is.

In 2009 March, as the Executive secretary of Mission Education, I participated at the Global Dalit Consultation in Bangkok organised by LWF and WCC. David Haslam and I were the only representatives from UK. The two of us managed to have a meeting at the House of the Lords in the Parliament House on 9th August 2009. This meeting paved the way for the formation of the Church Dalit Solidarity Group (CDSG) which continues to function enabling the Churches in UK to take a stand for the cause of Dalit Liberation. Initially CWM had these meetings and then it was held in different places. Now for more than a year the meetings are hosted by Rev Steve Pearce from the Methodist Church.

Embracing Dalit-Tribal Communities' aspirations
The PCI showed very keen interest in following up on the Dalit-Tribal communities coming together and working. Therefore, the Mission Education unit under the Community of Women and Men in Mission organised an event in Vishakhapatnam from 10th -15th March 2009 on the theme, "Engendering Theology from Dalit-Tribal Perspectives". This time, the Mission Education unit decided to bring together representatives from both Dalit and Tribal communities from Churches, Theological Colleges, Non- Governmental organisations, Christian organisations, and ecumenical organisations. We also had a few non-Christian participants. We opened up this consultation to people from

---

[7] Chhungi, Hrangthan. *Theologising Tribal Heritage: A Critical Relook*, CWM/ ISET/ECC/PCI/ISPCK, Delhi: 2008, pp. 311-319

beyond CWM member Churches so that both communities will be well represented. The participants during the group discussions identified the following areas as concerns on which the Dalit-Tribal communities can work together as these are faced by both communities – Struggle to reclaim their identities, overcome poverty, inadequate access to resources and Violence which they face frequently from the dominant groups.

The representatives from both communities were keen to extend solidarity to the other communities where their problems are not the same. Create and build solidarity forums as Dalit and Tribal forums, Demand for reservation as it is a common need, come together and build strong platforms economically and politically. Finally they also felt the need to build up awareness so that they become more aware of one another's concerns and issues.[8]

Expressing Faith in action through Mission Education

Mission Education unit wanted to follow up with the PCI led consultation's action plans by bringing together representatives from Orissa especially to address the issue of violence in Kandhamal and beyond. It was highly felt that if a true reconciliation and restoration of justice, identity and dignity should be achieved, then representatives from all sections of the society in Kandhamal/Orissa and from the national as well as International level be brought together. Participants came from the Dalit and Tribal communities in kandhamal and beyond including non -Christians, political leaders, lawyers, social organisations both Governmental and NGO's working with them, churches from among CWM members as well as beyond. We also had representatives from various Christian Organisations in India, Churches from NCCI and Trustee representatives from outside India United Welsh Independents (UWI), Wales and United Church Zambia (UCZ). It was a diverse group coming together to explore the possibilities of strengthening relationships between the Tribal and Dalit communities in Kandhmal so that they will be able to overcome the conspiracy of the Government, dominant castes and Multi-national

---

[8] For the Statement and action plan that came out of this consultation in please refer Appendix 8 in this book.

corporations which hand in gloves in order to exploit these poor Dalit-Tribal communities. What they want is the land that these people live in as it is very rich in minerals and to destroy these communities. They play the divide and rule policy and set up the Tribals and Dalits against each other to fight against each other and wipe themselves out. Kandhamal is not an isolated event as we see many other parts of India becoming a prey to this model of violence. So it is an urgent task here for us to act now so that peace becomes a reality in Kandhamal and beyond. This conspiracy is explained to the local communities comprising of Dalits and Tribals to bring peace.

As you read through the pages of this book, you will see how the dominant group's conspiracy is understood and how the Dalit-Tribal communities together with the support of the Church leadership at large and leaders from other faiths articulate their voice for restoring peace and justice in Kandhamal and beyond.

Our Hope: The language of Life to bring healing and wholeness
CWM began to address Dalit-Tribal issues extending a global and regional support from its inaugural Assembly of the new structure in 2003. The theme of that first assembly was 'Who is your Neighbour?' Nothing more could have witnessed to CWM responding to this theme than to express its total solidarity with Dalit-Tribal struggles for justice in India. In 2006, the theme 'Take home the good news' reiterated the commitment and passion for all member Churches to respond to the call of taking the gospel and the good news of Christ to their Churches, social contexts and homes especially people – individuals and communities suffering as justice was denied and deprived. This theme enabled us to look at those in the margins challenging us with Jesus' approach in meeting the man who lived in isolation away from his home, family, community and village. Whatever kept him away from people to run naked and cause destruction was stopped with Jesus' intervention. This theme Take home the good news has been thoroughly explored through the Daily Devotion Book 'Celebrating our diversities in God' edited, by Elizabeth Joy and published in 2008 by CWM bringing together rich Biblical reflections on the theme. Many contributions in this book are from Dalit-Tribal perspectives teasing out the theme from various perspectives from varied cultures, regions

and faith denominations to understand the need to take home the good news. Many pictures in this publication are also by Dalit and Tribal artists. The third Assembly of CWM in 2009 looked at the theme, 'Live the good news' taking the Samaritan Woman's story. This once again continued with the line of thought from 'Who is your neighbour?' to 'Take home the Good news' to 'Live the good news'.

Now that we have come yet to another new stage in CWM's life with it new promising structure with a new dynamic General Secretary Rev Dr Collin Cowan with his new staff team, I take this opportunity to wish him all the very best in every endeavour that he and his team envision and implement. I am indeed excited so much to see the new theme that will throw light on our present conditions, actions and future orientations.

So the very meaningful theme 'Hope: The language of life' will once again enable the CWM communities to continue their promises, support and solidarity to the Dalit-Tribal communities to experience Hope amidst all disillusionment. In and through Christ who stands out as our Hope, Faith and Love to create new and dynamic communities of hope and love let us experience God's reign. May we find a ray of hope turning into an array of hope with Christ's presence amidst us. May Jesus Christ, the saviour of the world who embraces all cultures, languages, regions, religions, faith denominations, communities cutting across all our short comings, challenges and changes that nurture discriminations and destructions, create a new heart, mind and soul that we may respond to his love on the cross that bears brings the greatest "hope; The language of life" amidst all realities that take us away from God's love.

Conclusion

This conference that was held in Bhubaneshwar, Orissa in January 2011 stands out as a very unique one where it is believed that for the first time an International ecumenical body visited both the Dalits and the Tribals. We are so very proud that PCI has translated its faith into action by sending a few of their missionaries to Kandhamal hospital, to the very heart of all violence that it has witnessed. However, it is indeed very encouraging to hear that after this particular event there in Orissa, Kandhamal had not witnessed any violence at least up until end of last year to my knowledge. I feel that the reopening of the Mission Hospital there that provides training and services to people – Dalits and Tribals, Christians and others brings in new hope for communities to experience healing and restoration of identity and dignity. I think this Hospital and its mission and ministry will be a promising factor to promote healing between the wounded communities.

I hope models like this will continue and also extend to various other parts of India which experience such violence based on faith, religion or any other cause. I am very proud of all the participants and resource persons at this consultation to bring Dalit-Tribal Interface: Healing and Restoration.... I am very proud to say that Rev Dr Collin Cowan the new General Secretary extends his full solidarity to the cause of Dalit-Tribal healing and wholeness and the theme 'Hope: The language of life' will resound with conviction promoting Faith and love at all levels in CWM communities and beyond.

I thank God profusely for giving me the wonderful opportunity to serve CWM. I am very grateful to God for God's richest grace and mercy that sustained me throughout my journey with CWM for eight years as the executive secretary of Mission Education unit. I also take this opportunity to thank every single person whom I got to meet and work with both at the office in London and every other part of the world. I hope and pray that we will commit ourselves as individuals and groups for the cause of Dalit-Tribal communities' healing and wholeness. May we ensure the following on the road to this healing and restoration of Hope, faith and Love through acts of justice which is the key for all transformation:

- Enduring and sharing the pain of Dalit-Tribal communities

- Empower Dalit-Tribal Communities through education

- Ensuring support to restore faith, hope and love

- Enable Dalit-Tribal communities to reclaim their identity and dignity

- Encourage Dalit-Tribal communities to move from margins to mainstream

- Equip Dalit-Tribal communities to take a lead role to witness their faith

- Eliminate exclusion, alienation and exploitation to let them live

- Experience the richness in the mutual sharing of faith, hope and love

Can we as Participants in God's Mission work with the Dalit-Tribal communities that struggle for justice to find healing and restoration of their identities and dignity? Can we extend our hearts and hands to empower, nurture and transform our local Churches, communities to reach out by affirming inclusive communities in Mission Network? I hope and pray that as you read through the pages of this book and look at the different perspectives from which the resource persons and participants address their solidarity with the Dalit-Tribal communities, you too will be inspired to join in and express your faith by giving 'A ray of hope' as you witness Christ's love for the entire world and mainly for the lost, least and the last. If we all join in to give just a ray of hope to the Dalit-Tribal communities in India and sub-continent through our faith in Christ, together, we will be able to make that an 'Array of hope' for them and also be mutually empowered with their experiences, witnessing and healing through restoration of their identities and dignity as total human beings created equally in God's image to lead a meaningful life in fellowship and friendship with all other communities including the oppressive ones. We achieve our target of giving hope as the language of life only when it is given to all communities and enable them to enrich the positive elements of their faiths which will then pave the way for each community to embrace every other community in love, faith and hope. We can restore healing only by celebrating our diversities be it gender, religion, region, culture or colour. Oppressive elements from every culture needs to give way for inclusive, transforming, sharing and caring values to build hopeful and loving communities.

Part II

PANEL PRESENTATIONS

The Search for Peace, Justice and Reconciliation

DR. JOHN DAYAL

Kandhamal and the rest of India wait for a lasting solution to anti-Christian violence. The involvement of Saffron Terror groups in triggering Kandhamal violence makes it a worrisome trend.

The violence against Christians in Kandhamal in 2007-2008, or indeed in Karnataka and elsewhere in India cannot be seen in isolation. It goes far beyond the simplistic preliminary assumptions of being a conflict between Dalits and Tribals over issues of forest land, or indeed the explosive and contentious argument, sometime voiced even by the Supreme Court, on conversions to Christianity. It is organically linked to the developments since the demolition of the Babri Masjid in Ayodhya on 6 December 1992, which polarised Indian society on religious lines, and enthused a right wing fundamentalism which has metamorphosed several times to now emerge in the form of what Congress General Secretary Digvijay Singh calls Saffron Terror. With its military connections and training, this goes even beyond the thuggery and mayhem of the Rashtriya Swayamsewak Sangh and its offshoots Vishwa Hindu Parishad, Bajrang Dal, Adivasi Kalyan Ashram and their siblings. Saffron Terror groups' hand has been seen in Kandhamal's violence by no less an agency than Military Intelligence of the Indian Armed Forces.

Saffron terror and the RSS groups of course derive their nurture from another stark reality of the Indian politico-cultural landscape. Sixty years after the People of India gave unto themselves a Constitution guaranteeing a Secular nation with government equidistance from all established religions, Muslims and Christians and even Sikhs have come face to face with a harsh reality – that India after 1992 does seem to have a "default" state religion, and that it is Hinduism, the religion of the majority. The Hindu ethos and its political compulsions permeate every facet of life – governance, the justice dispensation machinery, public institutions and economic and development processions. The assertion of identities in the complex of the caste matrix, confined not just to Hinduism, but aggressively percolating to Christianity and Islam, have collectively become a short-fuse to the powder keg of this nation of 1.2 billion people on the cusp of the second decade of the twenty-first century.

Communal violence trajectory

The starkness of the poverty statistics and inequity is counterpoised tragically with the comparative figures of death and devastation of Muslims and Christians butchered in two major pogroms in the last ten years – in 2002 in Gujarat and more recently in 2008 in the Kandhamal district of Orissa in a manifestation of cultural nationalism and xenophobia not seen since the bloodletting of the partition of India in 1947. The third set of statistics is the abysmal representation of the religious minorities in Parliament and legislative assemblies, in the higher echelons of the bureaucracy and the police, and most tellingly, on the Benches of the Supreme Court, the High Courts and the District and Sessions courts, where criminal justice is dispensed.

State Iniquity, Probity and Immunity

The Indian government is always shy of revealing the extent of inter religious violence, and it takes much goading to come anywhere near the truth. Official figures are half or a third of those spoken of by the victims communities or human rights organisations such as the United States Commission for International religious Freedom, Christian Solidarity Worldwide, the UN Special Rapporteur and Amnesty international. In a rare answer in the Upper House of Parliament, the Rajya Sabha, India's junior minister for home affairs, Ajay Maken reported there were at least 3,800 communal clashes rreported in India between 2004 and 2008, marking a steady rise over the years. The highest incidence of such violence in 2008 was reported from the eastern state of Orissa with 180 incidents, all against Christians, followed by the north-central state of Madhya Pradesh with 131, Uttar Pradesh state in the north with 114, western Maharashtra with 109 and Karnataka in the south with 108, half of them against Christians and the rest against Muslims. As per the total number of communal incidents in each state during the last five years, Maharashtra is on the top with 681 clashes, followed by Madhya Pradesh with 654 and Uttar Pradesh with 613.

Atrocities in Gujarat

Gujarat's anti Muslim violence in February-March 2002 shocked the nation and the world. The President and Prime minister of the time called it a blot on the cultural traditions of India. The government took more than three years to reveal its figures, sanitised most activists said immediately. The federal or Union government told Parliament that 790 Muslims and 254 Hindus were killed, 223 more people reported missing and another 2,500 injured. More than 100,000 people fled their homes. Human rights groups feared the toll to be as high as 2,000 Muslims killed.

The Guilty

The National Human Rights Commission (NHRC), an official body, found evidence of premeditation in the killings by members of extremist groups espousing Hindu nationalism, the Rashtriya Swayamsewak Sangh and its spawn, Vanvasi Kalyan Ashram, Vishwa Hindu Parishad and Bajrang Dal with a large doze of complicity by the State political and administrative apparatus headed by Gujarat chief minister Narendra Modi. Many Police officers were named in subsequent enquiry commissions for their role in the violence sparked by a fire on a train at the Godhra railway in Gujarat on 27 February 2002 in which 59 Hindu pilgrims were charred to death. Recently, a police officer said the Gujarat government had authorised the killing of Muslims after the riots, a charge the state government denies. This violence was marked by extraordinary barbarity, especially violence against women. The Supreme Court of India and special investigative teams are still investigating allegations of mass rape of women, including genital mutilation, the tearing out of foetus from pregnant women's bellies, and burning alive of entire families in their homes. Among the victims was a former Member of Parliament, a Muslim, who was burned alive. Another feature of the violence was the deliberate attempt to economically dis-empower the Muslim community. Their businesses, big and small, were meticulously targeted for arson. Several of these acts, mass arson, mutilation and rape would be later reflected against Christians in Kandhamal.

It is interesting to note that barring the occasional incident of retaliation, the Muslims were the overwhelming target, and yet in the arrests, while 27,901 Hindus were arrested, so were as many as 7,651 Muslims. In firing by the police, again, Muslims were the apparent target —93 Muslims were shot as also about 75 Hindus. Human Rights Watch criticized the Indian government for failure to address the resulting humanitarian condition of people, the "overwhelming majority of them Muslim," who fled their homes for relief camps in the aftermath of the events; as well as the Gujarat state administration for engaging in a cover-up of the state's role in the massacres. The violence spread to 151 towns and 993 villages in fifteen of the state's 25 districts as it raged unchecked between February 28 and March 3, and after a drop, restarted on March 15, continuing sporadically till mid June.

The Anti-Christian Violence

The violence in Orissa between 23 August and 1 October 2008 was comparatively on a much smaller scale, but was historically unique in being targeted against Christians. It differed from earlier anti Christian violence in its intensity and stark severity, sharing with Gujarat aspects of government complicity and an apparent free hand to the Hindutva Sangh Parivar. Almost for a month and a half, the district of Kandhamal, on a plateau in the midst of the state of Orissa, was out of bounds even to the government's troops while the killer gangs roamed the countryside, killing perhaps as many as a 100 people. **The government acknowledges 37 deaths – burning down 5,500 houses in about 400 villages, the destruction of 257 big and small Churches. As many as 55,000 people fled to the forest to save their lives, two thirds of them finally rescued in refugee camps set up by the government and guarded by Union forces.**

At the end of 2010, over 10,000 people had still not come back to their homes. Some left the place for good, seeking safety and jobs in other states. Many others had been barred from their villages by the Hindutva gangs which have openly declared that they will allow the Christians to return only on the condition they gave up their faith and converted to Hinduism. The government has continued to look on rather helplessly, as is evident to human rights activists and the international media who have seen how in the two fast track courts, a senseless justice is being meted out in which the killers have been let off in most of the cases because the killers have successfully forced all eyewitnesses to their crimes to renege in court.

Orissa chief minister Naveen Patnaik, who was in a coalition with the Bharatiya Janata party during the violence, and has since returned to power after severing relations with that party, has told the state legislature that the attacks were mainly led by right-wing outfits such as the Vishwa Hindu Parishad and its youth wing Bajrang Dal. The chief minister's indictment of his organisations connected with his former political allies is the first such confirmation of the involvement of these hyper nationalistic groups in violence against religious minorities. Recent revelations by Military intelligence point to the role of the so called Saffron or Hindutva Terror Groups which were also responsible for several acts of bomb blasts and murders in Ajmer Sharif, the Indo Pakistani Samjhauta Express and the Moti Masjid of Hyderabad.

Society has changed, and with it civil society too

There is a classic contradiction of the average Hindu, villager, urban lumpen, middle class, even the billionaires of Indian Inc., feeling vulnerable and cornered on the one hand, and on the other hand increasingly intolerant of religious minorities, particularly Muslims and Christians which are now branded even in academic circles as "Non-Indic' faith groups, a term unheard of before 1992, and reluctant therefore to concede any further rights or favours to them. Recent cross-border terrorism, the rise of Al Qaeda, the unrelenting vicious circle of military and police atrocities, disobedience and mass secessionist violence in the Kashmir valley, all tend to reinforce the contemporary Hindu middle class and civil society stance against Islam and Muslims. And by extension it is carried over against Christians whose tenuous linkages with the British Raj are periodically paraded under the sun in a name-and-shame exercise whenever there is a demand for more rights by that micro-minority.

Conversions

It is also clear that concepts of secularism have changed. The Supreme Court of India under Chief Justice J S Verma said Hindutva was a "way of life" and could not be equated with "narrow fundamentalist Hindu religious bigotry." The Supreme Court's failing to, or refusing to, define religions, especially Hinduism and its differentiation from the ideological aspects of Hindutva has had deep implications. Structured institutions such as the subordinate courts and the National Commission for Minorities thereafter have not been able to reach conclusions on critical issues such as conversions, specially forced conversions to Hinduism of Adivasi-Tribals and marginalised Christians under the use of Ghar wapsi, a return home. Social psychologist Ashish Nandy and others raise the fear that minorities will now have to, "for good or worse," prepare to protect themselves. His worst case scenario is that this is creating a new breeding ground for terrorism with, inevitably, the state crackdown and violence.

Solutions and Structures

The established Church and the so called political leadership of the community had felt afraid even to admit to the violence against it. The established Church finds itself cornered, partly because of its need to project the large number of educational and medical institutions it runs and which can be put under pressure either by the majority community or by the state apparatus as Bishops have found in the past sixty years. This also is the reason why the Church has not been able to successfully articulate the development needs of the Christian community, the many ways its progress has been hindered in the past years. In fact, there is no collective statement made by the Church impressing on the government to focus attention on the economic development of a micro-minority which has given to the nation so much in important fields of education and medicare.

This creates a major crisis – the Christian legislators are silent because they have not been elected by a Christian constituency, and the disunited Church finds itself powerless and therefore unwilling to take up issues and rake up controversies. The collective structural silence is deafening.

A small group of Christians has been trying to rouse the Planning Commission of India and the national government on these issues, with very mixed results. The Planning Commission allocates funds and sets yardsticks for the allocation of government resources to various segments of society in the states, and the Christian community fears it has not been given a fair hearing. Some issues are singular to us, because of demographic dispersal and disempowerment in some spheres, especially those concerning Dalit Christians. Even among minorities, governmental action and proactive developmental activity has been uneven. Compared to other minorities – the Muslims are five times as many, and the Sikhs, for instance, are concentrated in Punjab and therefore exercise considerable political power at the national level – Christians have been on the margins of political consciousness of the governments in power over the decades, and especially in recent years.

Test surveys by the All India Catholic Union and the All India Christian Council show that the Christian community in reality lacks an upper middle class other than in Goa, Mumbai and Kerala, does not have an entrepreneurial class, and there is little self-employment amongst our youth, particularly among the Dalits, the rural communities. There is vast under- employment amongst educated youth in urban areas. The National Minorities Development Finance Corporation has failed singularly in reversing poverty and unemployment. The Christian community has done no formal survey to gauge the social and economic infirmity of the people, and particularly of the youth, in the hinterland. Christians have allowed the growth of myths about their economic status based on the images of a few well off people from Goa, Bombay, Kerala or the metropolitan areas of Delhi and Calcutta. The vast majority of Christians amongst the Dalits in Tamil Nadu and Andhra, the Tribals in central and East India, and the Dalits and others in the Punjab and Uttar Pradesh are amongst the most economically deprived.

At the turn of the second decade, security of Religious Minorities remains a dominant one. The Christian community had felt itself very safe in India at the dawn of Independence, and the formative years of the democracy under Jawaharlal Nehru, and then under the premiership of Lal Bahadur Shashtri, Indira Gandhi and Rajiv Gandhi. But after a spurt of violence in 1998-1999, hate crimes against the Church and the Christian community have been increasing alarmingly since 1997, averaging about 250 incidents a year. But 2007 and 2008 have seen such violence reach an unprecedented level. The violence has not been confined to Orissa. Fourteen other States have been affected, seven seriously. Karnataka is now second only to Orissa in crimes against Christians. Battalions of Central forces are needed to maintain peace, and yet a sense of deep insecurity still permeates the community in Orissa. The situation in Chhattisgarh is also getting out of hand, very rapidly.

The Catholic Union and the Christian Council, which are the vocal community groups active in human rights, have called on the Union Government that it must carry out a full investigation into the nationwide activities of extremist groups accused of the incitement and perpetration of violence against minority groups, including Hindutva groups, their foreign finances, and their penetration into the administrative and police apparatus. Orissa particularly brings urgency to the demand of enforcing rule of law, ending Impunity of state, Police and criminal justice dispensation system in assuring freedom of faith: In State after State, the community has watched in utter helplessness uniformed Policemen accompany assailants attacking institutions, Churches and house Churches. In States such as Manipur, even villages have dared pass laws against Christians, banning conversions and excommunicating people. Pastors and Priests have been arrested on false charges, denied bail, and harassed. Often, the police have stood by while Priests, pastors and Lay persons were beaten up, often in the glare of Television cameras. The Subordinate magistracy and judiciary have often been partisan in their conduct. This impunity must end.

It is only now that the Christian community has started seeking redress of economic deprivation and reversal of unemployment and under-employment amongst Christian youth, stressing the need for a National Commission on the lines of the Justice Rajender Sachhar

Commission set up for Muslims to survey and assess the quantum of deprivation, marginalisation and lack of devolution of developmental initiatives, to the Christian community. There is over eight per cent joblessness amongst Christian youth, the highest among minorities. Tribal Christian girls are amongst the most deprived in terms of education and nourishment. Rural employment generation schemes and central special components for marginalised groups do not reach their Christian counterparts in Tribal and rural India There is no real assessment as to what extent institutions such as the National Minorities Financial Development Corporation, or sundry scholarship schemes have benefitted the Christian community even if they may have benefited some other Minorities. Government is at last under some pressure to ensure fair spending on a pro rata basis on the Christian community from schemes meant to benefit the minority communities. Dalits, Tribals, Landless labourers and marginal farmers, coastal and fishery workers and urban youth remain major victims.

The ironically titled Freedom of Religion Bills actually erodes the Constitutional right to Freedom to profess, practice and propagate faith. They have become instruments of persecution, and in fact, provide an excuse for criminal and communal elements to target the Church and Christian workers in particular when they exercise their right to propagate their faith. The community is now demanding that Government must assure there will be no effort in the future to infringe upon, erode, or nibble at Minority educational and other Constitutional rights under any pretext. Activists are also pointing to the shrinking of what they describe as the Secular-Spiritual Space.

In the light of past experience, the community response to the government's proposal to bring forward a bill for an Equal Opportunity commission has been met by some anxiety. The existing institutions such as the national Human Rights commission and the National Commission for Minorities have been seen as not really helping the people, and yet another central body created without community participation can hardly be expected to invoke confidence.

In an overview, it is quite clear that an environment of suspicion marks the relationship between the federal and provincial governments and their institutions and agencies on the one hand, and the two major religious minorities, the Muslims and the Christians. But it is quite clear that the search for justice and reconciliation cannot be by ignoring the critical need for justice, reparations, rehabilitation. The peace of a graveyard will be no solace to religious minorities.

Causes for Kandhamal Violence

FR. AJOY SINGH

1. Hindutiva's Hate campaigns

Conversion is a crime and Christians are anti-national. The Spread of canard through sishu mandirs, schools and false rumours such as land grabbing, beef eating, caste certificate, killing of swami by Christians

- The submissive Hindu who had been hitherto terrorised by the Christian missionaries began to assert himself. Hindu jaage, Christi bhaage became a popular slogan of the Vanvasis of Dangs.

- The success of this campaign like the one led by Swami Laxmanananda in Kandhamal enraged the anti-Hindu forces.

  Laxmanananda : The innocent Hindus were shocked and had one question: Who will rescue us from such religious terrorism? But nobody was there to answer. When the Hindus of the Kandhamal district and other tribal-dominated districts of Orissa were suffering from the inhuman acts and conversion bids of Christian missionaries, they got a little ray of hope. A saffron-clad saint Swami Laxmananda Saraswati reached there as the nemesis of all the missionary activities

- Shri Indresh Kumar, Member, RSS National Executive, said that conversion is a sin and a crime against God and it must come to an end in order to maintain peace and tranquillity in the world. Unless and until the church-sponsored conversion is stopped, peace and brotherhood cannot be established in this world. That book points out how more than 100 civilisations were destroyed and 1.5 crore people have been killed by the church in the whole world. He urged the government to publish a white paper on church funds and its utilisation for the development of backward people and why the church fails to bring development in the underdeveloped areas, under its exclusive operation.

- Open letter to Pope: Patron and Convener of Himalaya Pariwar, Friends of International Society and Nationalist Muslim Forum, Shri Indresh Kumar, wrote an open letter to the Pope Benedict XVI requesting him to do away with the service activities being done by the Christian missionaries with the motive of converting people to Christianity. Conversion to Christianity in the pretext of service, health, education and co-operation is an insult and devaluation to the service itself and a crime against humanity. He further said that in all the states, districts, areas, where Christian missionaries are active and powerful, the hatred, crime, social unrest, separatism, addiction are on the increase and the environment of peace, harmony, brotherhood and happiness is fading away. He asked the Pope, "Would you like to accept this face of Christianity?"

- Subash Chouhan, Bajrang Dal state convenor, indicts, *"There is so much cow slaughter, for example in Sundargarh, Bhadrak, thousands of cows. We believe that the cow is our mother, but they want to kill the cow. So, if necessary we will use a suicide squad. To save the country and its* sanskriti *[culture], we will do whatever is necessary."*(February-March 2004 Year 10   No.96, Special Report, Communal Combat)

- Swami Aseemanand, one of the key instigators of the Kumbh, believes the Shabri Kumbh Mela will '...end missionary activity in Dangs'. In 1999 Aseemanand told the Times of India, 'Dangs cannot know peace so long as even a single tribal remains Christian.'

2.   Abdication of State responsibility
Saffronisation of government machinery: Impunity and protection to the sangh violent journey in nexus with the administration

POTENTIAL LAW & ORDER: COMMUNAL

* The district share of population of Christians is on steady increase which has now reached 15% (as per 1991 Census). There is resistance of the activities of missionaries in some areas like under Town, Kotagarh, Balliguda, Sarangada, Phiringia PS areas. Due to this recent development there is ill-feeling and tension on communal line at the village level.

* The post criminal activities by both communities in brief are as follows: During period from 28.11.86 to 9.2.87 Ratha Yatra was organised by Swami Laxmanananda Saraswati of Chakapad Ashram under Tikabali PS, it resulted in heightened tension and registration of following number of cog. Cases. Cog. Cases registered : 38, No. of Churches burnt : 18 (source: *http:// kandhamal.nic.in/km-admn/km-spk.htm#LAW*)

* Raikia Church 2004, Kattiniga burning-1984

* April 8-10th 2006: Singhal said conversion is not only a crime but is weakening the country as a whole. In order to protect the Hindu religion, we have to give burial to all other religions and called for reconversion with single heart and mind in the presence of RSS chief, 15 Orissa ministers and administration

3.   Outside Traders

Assertive and economically better off Adivasi and Dalit community a threat to Outside traders schema of exploitation and subjugation. Control of resources: There is corporate nexus caste lobby; Natural resources at galore. Bamunigam shops attacked.

4.   Caste system

Rise of Indigenous communities a threat to dominant upper caste, traders and government machinery nexus: Brahminic economical order. They act like villains providing all logistic support

5.   Politicisation: Gujarat model

With Modi triumphant, an emboldened Sangh is set upon doing a repeat of Gujarat, reports **S. ANAND**

"You are just burning tyres. How many Isai houses and churches have you burnt? Without kranti (revolution) there can be no shanti (peace). Narendra Modi has done kranti in Gujarat, the reason why shanti's there."

Lakhanananda Saraswati, 82-year-old Sangh leader inciting his followers on his cell phone on December 25, from a medical centre in Daringbadi, Kandhamal district, in the presence of police and journalists: *From Tehelka Magazine, Vol 5, Issue 2, Dated Jan 19, 2008*

6.   Media role

- In the context of the Kandhamal riot, the media committed a major mistake by doing a wrong analysis of the basic facts regarding the district.

- Kandhamal - the Oriya media has played a very narrow, irresponsible and unprofessional role. Facts and information have, many times, been dished out to provoke the public.

- These were not meant to establish the truth behind the communal carnage in Kandhamal, rather to help wipe out the minorities of the District. Sufferings and traumas of the riot-victims hardly found space in the Media.

- What happened in Kandhamal after Laxmananda's killing was not a riot; it was, literally a genocide. In riot, both parties have some role to play. But in Kandhamal the minority was at the receiving end. More than 50 people were killed; more than 25 thousand Christians became refuges in their own land. But Sangh Parivar played a cruel joke on them when it declared in a number of Press conferences in Bhubaneswar that Hindus in Kandhamal were the worst oppressed lot. Media, without enquiring into the veracity of this statement, published it. On the other hand, TV channels were trying to prove that whatever was happening in Kandhamal was natural and consequences of the Hindu sentiment.

- Media had no word of sympathy for riot victims of Kandhamal. Rather, they were more concerned that the killers and conspirators of Laxmananda not yet apprehended. However, this whole theory of "killers and conspirators" was manufactured by Sangh Parivar. It has categorically blamed the minority community for the killing. So, it is duty of Hindus to wipe out the minority community. Thousands of leaflets have been distributed by Sangh Parivar all across the state with this message. Their leaders were uttering the same line in meetings. Unfortunately, media offered more space to these statements!

7.   Unprepared Church's Response: Ignorant and Frightened
This issue needs to be relooked by the church for further discussion.

Dalit – Tribal Interface:
Healing and Restoration

BISHOP SAMSON DAS

The term 'Adivasi' or 'Original Settlers' or 'First settlers' refers to groups of people who are categorized by the four characteristics given below:

*   Geographical isolation

*   Backwardness

*   Distinctive culture, language and religion

*   Shyness of contact

A large percentage of Indians and almost 30% of the population of Orissa are Adivasi. They fall in the brackets of Schedule Tribes. The term 'Dalit' on the other hand refers to castes as set down by the Indian Government. The Dalits are communities from lower and backward classes who have been exploited, marginalized and never been given a chance to enter into the main stream of society for centuries in the past by the dominant upper castes and trader communities. Since India gained her Independence, the government has recognized this and tried to infuse steps to try and bring these two communities into the mainstream by introducing a host of benefits for them starting from education to reservation in jobs. At the ground level, realities are different. The Adivasi and Dalits continue to be oppressed, exploited and displaced. Atrocities against them by the upper castes, the money lenders and traders, the police force and most recently by right wing extremist groups and Hindu fundamentalist groups continue.

Orissa houses 5,77,775 Muslims and 6,20,000 Christians, 5.1 Million Dalits from 93 caste groups and over 7 million Adivasis from 62 tribes. Around 87% of Orissa's population lives in villages. Nearly half the population lives in poverty. Almost a quarter of the state's population is Advasis, of which 68.9% are impoverished, 66% illiterate and 2% have completed education. 59.9% of the Dalits live in poverty.

The Dalits and Adivasis have never been the part of the conventional trade systems in India. In today's scenario, the principles of globalization, liberation and privatization have proved to be hostile and detrimental to the livelihood and existence of the indigenous people of India.

The Adivasis are basically forest dwellers and have a strong bond with the forest eco-system. This relationship is endangered because of industrialization and globalization. The Adivasis are displaced from their homes and their environment in order to accommodate industrialization and urbanization. The Government along with the forest department has been dispossessing the forest based Adivasis under the pretext of forest conservation and wild life protection. On the contrary on the same locations we find government establishments of defense projects, bio-experiments and eco-tourism.

Issues that need to be addressed:

- The indigenous people are thrown out of their resource zones and livelihood. As a result their life style, culture and eco-friendly ethos are reversed.

- The Government of India does not clearly define the rights of the indigenous groups to land, forests and water. Many so called developmental projects have resulted in the mass displacement and migration of these people to other areas.

- All other production based communities have a minimum right to enter the market but the indigenous people have no right to market. As a result their trade, profession, market and livelihood suffers.

- The corporate houses need resources and the people need their livelihood; it is a war between surplus and survival.

Recently the Kandhamal riots saw an attack on Christians mainly belonging to the 'Pano' community. Some historians labeled it as purely an ethnic conflict between the Adivasi and Dalits. It is true that there was simmering tension between the two communities, Panos who are Dalits and Kondhas who are Tribals. However, the Hindu fundamentalist groups took advantage of this situation and inflamed the issue to large proportions.

In the aftermath of the brutal killing of Swami Lakhamananda Saraswati, a mindless mayhem of violent atrocities has been unleashed against the Christians in Orissa. Since 24th Aug 2008, mobs belonging to Hindu fundamentalists' organizations have been on the rampage; attacking, plundering and destroying Churches and property as well as savagely murdering many Christians. Heart breaking incidents of tortures and attacks on Christians have been reported to the media. The Government authorities seem to have turned a deaf ear to the cry of the suffering and persecuted and are hesitant to take any positive measures to pacify the situation. The Chief Minister of Orissa, Mr. Naveen Patnaik made a statement in the media that the problem was more ethnic and sectarian in nature than communal. But facts are otherwise.

It has been alleged by the Sangha Parivar that the **conversion** is the root cause of riots of Kandhamal. However, visiting the violence-hit Kandhmal, the National Commission of Minorities Members enquired from District Officials and from the State Secretariat whether any case of conversion had been reported or filed with regard to infringement of Orissa Freedom of Religion Act, which bans forcible and fraudulent conversions and has been in existence for decades. The commission could not get even a single case. If there is not a single violation of the Law of the Land why was there such a commotion, so much hatred and such brutal violence? The republic of India, which is constitutional and secular, is posed with critical questions – **whether its citizens are free to profess a religion of their choice or not?**

There is absolutely no evidence to back up the VHP's claims that Missionaries have forcibly converted large number of tribal folk. What the communal outfits are targeting is the freedom of conscience and the right freely to process, practice and propagate religion guaranteed as fundamental right in Article 25 of the Indian Constitution. What is being witnessed in the name of re-conversion in Orissa is the attempt by Fascist forces to convert Tribals to Hinduism. The attack on Pano converts to Christianity is aimed at terrorizing them into submission.

Let us remember what Jawaharlal said, "Those who want to attack the minorities will have to do so over my dead body". Communal atrocities such as those in Orissa, Gujarat and elsewhere have to be viewed, first and foremost, from the perspective of national integration and our collective need to create a peaceful and terror free society. Gandhiji's commitment to the freedom and integrity of India made him give priority to national unity. He knew that the truth alone could be the foundation for that unity. So he proclaimed "Truth is God". Terror is the opposite of truth.

Statistics of Death and Destruction in the anti-Christian Violence during 24th Aug – 30th October 2008

Districts affected	14
Villages looted and destroyed	300
Houses burnt	4100
People rendered homeless	50000
People murdered	57
Fathers/Pastors/Nuns injured after attacks	10
Refugees in relief camps	22,236
Men, Women and Children injured	18,000
Churches destroyed	104
Schools and Colleges destroyed	13

What are the reasons behind Hindu-Christian Violence?

The minority Christian community in Kandhamal district many of whom are Forest Tribal people and Low Caste Dalits converts from Hinduism to Christianity say they have been targeted by radical Hindu nationalist's organization seeking to put an end to the church and its activities in the region.

Village after village along the forested roads of this remote high land district lie in ruins. But the tribal Hindu community says that the Christians are to be blamed with their provocative demands for the same preferential access to jobs, education and land that the tribal and low caste Hindu communities receive.

Proposals or suggestions that can be implemented

- Firstly we must understand that globalization does not necessarily mean development. Secondly trade and financial liberalization does not raise social and labor standards.

- Policies which create employment and raise productivity, especially in the agriculture and natural resource sector can be implemented.

- Two–folded campaigns must be launched. Firstly to recognize and support the identity, culture and rights of the indigenous people. Secondly against the politics of free trade, trade related policies and the market-economy at large.

- Plans must be chalked out so that the Adivasis can benefit from forest use, maintain their cultural identity and achieve adequate levels of livelihood.

- Whenever right to land is not recognized, it leads to land alienation. This can lead to upheaval and contradiction in the socio-economic order of the Adivasis.

- Call for Satbhavana Meeting with Hindu brethren for dialogue and better relationship in order to maintain communion and solidarity with them.

- We must realize that our well-being doesn't not entirely depend on Police or our own strategies, but on our neighbors. With friendly relationship with all in the village, the non – Christian families will protect us. We have witnessed this in Kandhamal. We need Local, National and International support. Therefore, publishing relevant and correct information to the general public, media, funding agencies, Government Agencies, etc is very essential.

- Communication Cell of the church establishment should gather useful information from different places, share the data information with others and make them available to the Government authorities.

- Keep good relationship with the Press, Media, T. V channels, Networks, etc. we need their support. We can also challenge a particular News Paper in the Press Council of India if the paper reports falsely.

- We should avoid disrespectful comments about other religions at all times.

- Our language and vocabulary is at times absolute and exclusivist in nature. Often we use military and warfare language such as "Army", "Advance", "Attack", "Battle", "Campaign", "Crusade" and "Penetration". Sometimes while referring to our friends and neighbors of other faiths and neighbors of their faiths we use words like "Pagan", "Living in darkness", "Heathen" and "Gentiles". Our language and approach should be sober and loving. The aggressive attitude of Christians continues to keep the Churches away from the main stream of Indian Culture and Political Life as a community.

In fact it is through education, health services and developmental activities rendered by the missionaries the Dalits and the Tribals have entered into the main stream of the society. Their all round development is becoming a challenge to Sangh Parivar and to the dreaded Caste System, which has kept them for centuries under their hegemony. The empowerment of the marginalized threatens the vested interests of the upper classes. For generations, Tribals and the so called "untouchables" have been kept down. Christian missionaries, with their stress on education and health, have challenged the foundations of this Social Order. The history of conversions in India to Christianity is predominantly a history of the untouchable and excluded communities converting from their excluded status to accessing social mobility and educational rights.

In order to understand the furors which have been raised up by the issue of conversion we must understand its socio political implications.

1.   *The Church must recognize the socio – political implications of conversion*

In the minds of those who oppose conversion the issue is primarily socio-political than theological. Rather the Hindu voice has been raised as a reaction against attacks on Indian culture, values, standards, tradition etc. Their assumption is that the followers of Christianity and Islam have extra – terrestrial loyalties. They say that we owe allegiance to foreign powers and this allegiance supersedes our allegiance to our own nation. Mass conversions among Dalits and Tribals, where large numbers turn to Christianity on a single day, have more socio–political connotations than religious. Dalit Conversions are more of political statements than religious. Conversion is seen as a demonstration of the empowerment of Dalits and therefore it is a challenge to the oppressive forces that kept them in bondage for centuries.

2.   *The Church must rethink its Theology of Mission*

Unfortunately, some Missions in India operate on the basis of many unbiblical assumptions and patterns. The concern for Mission in the Bible is closely associated with the concern for the Glory of God. Sadly, the practice of Mission has become dominated by the influence of social sciences and management savvy techniques. I have heard of an American Missionary leader who while talking to church planters said that Pepsi and Coke have managed to find a presence in every village of India, whereas the Gospel hasn't. When souls are equated with Pepsi and Coke, it is natural that management and marketing principles creep into our projection of the Gospel.

3.   *The Church must reject Social Service as a means of gaining converts*

Both evangelism and social service have been integral part of Christian Mission. However, using medical, educational and other developmental services merely to attract converts will be wrong on the part of the Church. We need to avoid two extremes here. Christian social service is just not philanthropy but a part of Christian witness. This is not because we want to take credit for the work we are doing. The obligation upon Christians is not just to show compassion but to show it in the name of Christ. On the other hand, when acts of compassion are turned into "baits" for grabbing converts then it is totally unbiblical. We should show compassion selflessly in the name of Christ without expectations of returns for church growth.

Healing and Restoration: Towards Peace, Justice and Reconciliation among Dalit and Tribal Communities – Endeavours of the NCCI

REV DR ROGER GAIKWAD

On 20th and 21st November 2008, a Dalit-Tribal Interface was facilitated, in the backdrop of the Kandhamal Carnage, by the National Council of Churches in India (NCCI) at Nagpur. This interface came out with a mission statement. Among other things, the Statement asserted:

> "The grave concern that offshoots from the saga of violence in Orissa is the rift between Pano Dalits and the Khand Tribals,- the indigenous people of this land who share the common ethos and culture. With the advent of the outsiders into this land, Khand Tribals have been hinduised and Pano Dalit have been Christianised, and in recent years religion happened to be the conflicting element in this region and a whole series of violence in Orissa has taken the religious flavour to it."

Quoting the prayer of Jesus in John 17:21, "That they may all be one", the Statement goes on to say:

- Therefore we as people of God, call on both the Dalits & Tribals to give up conflicts among them and seek unity and cooperation in their joint struggle for liberation.

- We urge the two communities, if issues like land , culture, reservation & conversion happen to be the core issues that have been dividing the indigenous people, let these issues be addressed

PART II: PANEL PRESENTATIONS

on an indigenous table and not on a religious table, which thus far has been so.

- We call on the religions and religious people to withdraw from flaring up ongoing conflict among these communities, and let a continuous Dalit-Tribal interface be organised, so that the issues can be spelt out, addressed and solved.

- We request the role of the civil society, responsible citizens and the interfaith communities for they need to initiate such interfaces among Dalits and Tribals for they share many things in common. Such interfaces will give an opportunity to work out the convergences between the two communities, to express their divergences and to work out creatively strategies that can sustain the indigenous nature of these communities.

- We call on all our churches to intervene in getting the schemes and provisions given by the governments to the Dalits & Tribals in our respective communities.

From the above extract, it is very clear that the NCCI has advocated the stand that since some of the *Panos* and *Khands* are divided on the basis of religion, the latter cannot play the primary role in bringing about peace, justice and reconciliation among them. **The bonding factor is their realization that both of them are the indigenous peoples of the region.** There ought to be mutual respectful recognition that they are both the inhabitants of the land. Therefore, they should not allow the outsider to take over their land, their society and culture and to exploit them economically and to manipulate their relationships under the garb of religious communalism. Both Dalits and Tribals are marginalized communities in society. So if they fight among themselves then both of them stand to lose. It is like superpowers (first world countries and MNCs) secretly instigating conflicts/wars between two third world and/or neighbouring countries, accruing orders from the latter for their own arms (weapons) industry, and making the two countries economically dependent on these super powers, while these latter publicly pose themselves as international peace brokers and policemen.

A second important feature of the Mission Statement calls upon religions and religious people to desist from communal conflicts. As such, as has been asserted again and again by theologians and religious leaders, **in general no religion ever preaches hatred towards adherents of other religious traditions. It is the fundamentalist and communal interpretations of religious beliefs and practices that cause problems in inter-community relationships.** For example, in many creation/origin myths and folklore of several indigenous communities which grew in relative isolation from one another, the first human beings are those of one's own particular community. As each community gradually came into social contact with people of other communities, their understanding of 'human being' underwent changes and their creation/origin myths also needed to be reinterpreted. If these stories were not interpreted in a spirit of either tolerance or ecumenism, it gave rise to ethnic hostility and conflict. One particular community then considers itself the rightful inhabitant of a particular region and looks at others as usurpers. Even if the neighbouring communities may follow the same or similar religion and culture, they may still consider one another as enemies. There are instances in some places where ethnic blood has proved to be 'thicker' than baptismal water, and therefore one community has fought with another community over the issue of right of habitation in, and ownership and commercial use of a particular region.

Hence there is the need for on-going intra-community and inter-community dialogical relationships. The NCCI has been engaged in facilitating such relationships. At the same time, the church and society has to be conscientized/sensitized about the trans-religious factors and forces that politicize and communalize religion, culture and society. The NCCI Commissions on Tribals and Adivasis; Dalits; Justice, Peace and Creation; and on Policy, Governance and Public Witness have been engaged in such ministries. Consultations on topics such as "The Rights of the Tribal and Adivasi in India: An Appraisal from the Perspectives of Theological and Indian Constitutional Rights", "Sustainable Development and Empowerment of Tribal Women", "Violence and Violation of Human Rights: Patterns and Perspectives for Peace", etc. The NCCI has also been engaged in political advocacy, prophetic conversations, proclamation concerns, progressive networking and partnership building ministries.

A third important concern in the mission statement is **the responsibility placed upon the church, inter-faith communities and civil society to initiate and strengthen Dalit-Tribal interfaces**. However the tragedy is that the caste factor still plays an important role inside the Church. Caste is still a decisive factor in elections to positions of power in some churches, in marriages, and in the formation of some congregations. So also stereotypes about tribal Christians regarding their cultural practices, their economic situation, etc., impede their fuller participation in the life of the wider church and society. If such is the case how can Tribal-Dalit interfaces be expedited and encouraged? The Commission on Dalits has last year, through its national ecumenical conference, come out with a statement which begins with the slogan, "No one can serve Christ and Caste!" The emphasis of the NCCI has been on "Churches being and effecting to be Just and Inclusive Communities." The previous year, that is, in 2009, the theme of the Dalit Liberation Sunday was: **"Crossing Boundaries and Building Bridges: Overcoming Prejudices."** The Commission on Tribals and Adivasis has time and again called for the integration of indigenous communities with dignity rights and empowerment in the society. The challenge before the NCCI, in keeping with its centenary year (2014) theme, is "Towards integral mission and grass root ecumenism." The Tribal-Dalit interface has to be facilitated at the grass roots. Local churches need to be stirred and encouraged to practice ecumenism of all kinds (denominational, gender, social, etc.), thereby integrating Dalits and Tribals together with the Church and Society.

It should also be remembered that, **in most Indian religious and cultural traditions, 'hospitality' to others, particularly to the stranger/ foreigner/ (a person outside one's community) has been a cherished virtuous practice. This quality has been integrated with the religion and culture of indigenous communities**. (Sad to say, this virtue has often been exploited by the commercial-minded outsider.) It is this quality that has to be strengthened. In January 2010, the Youth Commission of the NCCI organized a national ecumenical youth assembly on the theme, "Come, Let's be Friends". Yes, in the Dalit-

Tribal Interface, among other things, what is important is that we would be friends in solidarity, in suffering and in struggles for the values of the reign of God on earth.

Let us move from interface to integration!

Church's Response for "Healing and Restoration Towards, Peace and Reconciliation for Dalit and Tribal Communities"

REV.LALDAWNGLIANA

At the outset I would like to mention that the incidents at Kandhamal had a great impact shocking the Christian population in North East India, particularly the sufferings it caused on the people of Kandhamal. Although many of the Churches have their programmes for the restoration of peace I would like to focus on the Presbyterian Church of India (PCI) from within the North East India. The General Assembly of the PCI has eight synods with the population of a little over 12 lakhs, who are mostly spread in the North East India, while a few members are scattered in other parts of India. Extending the Kingdom of God is PCI's main programme, in which direct evangelism has been regarded as the most effective one. All the synods have freedom of administration in Pastoral ministry, and Mission engagement, but all synods are guided together by one Constitution of the General Assembly of the PCI.

Programmatic response of the PCI in relation to the Kandhamal Violence

1.   Immediately after the incidents at Kandhamal during Christmas, 2007 the General Assembly, Presbyterian Church of India released a statement about the situation and requesting all Christian communities to pray for restoration of normal situation in the

area, and also for the comfort of the suffering and the bereaved families who lost their loved ones during these incidents. As such all the churches within the General Assembly of the Presbyterian Church that stretched out within the different states of North East India prayed together for the normalcy of the situation.

2. Peace Rally: On the 7th September, 2008 under the proposal of the Mizoram Synod, a state-wide prayer programme was organized in which a relief fund of almost Rs 10 lakhs was collected. The Joint Mizoram Churches in Mizoram organized Peace March in all the district headquarters and capital of Mizoram on 29th Sept, 2008 to show solidarity with the suffering Christians who were tortured in different parts of India and in particular the Kandhamal district. The Khasi Jaintia Presbyterian Assembly also organized an interfaith Peace Prayer Programme in the KJP Assembly Hall in which all faith communities in Shillong attended and prayed together for the peaceful atmosphere in the Kandhamal area. A peace rally was organized in Shillong city on the 4th of November 2008, to address the issue of such violence, in which members from other faiths like Buddhism and Hinduism participated. The participants felt sorry for the incidents and had a mass prayer so that such incidents may not happen again, but an understanding among the faith groups in the Orissa State may enable them to exist together in peace and harmony. The rally appealed that such incidents among the faith communities would not erupt again in the region.

3.   PCI Office representatives met Mr. L. K. Advani, the Leader of the Opposition in the Parliament of India at that time, when he visited Shillong and submitted a letter urging him to act to towards the quick restoration of peace and maintain tranquility in the state.

4. With the intention to address disharmony and social issues that affect and endanger the tranquility of the region (North East India) as well as the entire country, the General Assembly, PCI works together with the Forum called 'The Joint Peace Mission Team' (JMPT), with Roman Catholic, Council of Baptist Church

in North East India, Church Auxiliary for Social Action, and North East India Christian Council. So the JMPT organized a Goodwill Group visit to Kandhamal and shared Christian love for healing of the trauma experienced by them during the incidents in Kandhamal.

5.   Recently the Mizoram Synod has decided to initiate a mission work by sending a missionary doctor to Orissa. It is expected that this initiative will pave the way for the Mizoram Synod involvement in a greater scale in this State.

6.   In recent years the PCI General Assembly, has decided to respond to issues related with violence and problems that hindered the harmony of people, through its Peace and Justice Committee which was adopted in 2006. This Committee takes up issues of Ethnic conflicts, disaster management, relief and rehabilitation, economic exploitation, human rights violations in various forms and related matters to peace and justice. It also takes up preventive measures to thwart the design for denying Peace and Justice by campaign, training, seminars, consultation etc. The General Assembly also particularly decided to respond to the issues that relates with the atrocities against Christians within and outside the country. These programmes are intended not only for implementation within the region but also can be made available as and when necessary to any other place beyond India.

Conclusion

Most of the inhabitants of the North East India are Tribals and in fact, the response made by the Churches in North East India has never really focused on the issues of Tribals or Dalits per se. however, the basic concern here is the torturing of the Christians in the Kandhamal area irrespective of their ethnic group. I would like to mention here that I believe strongly that this programme will lead us to a better as well as a deeper understanding of the issues leading us to the restoration of Peace and Harmony for Dalits and Tribals of the Kandhamal with all its complexity.

Healing and Restoration Towards Peace, Justice and Reconciliation of Dalit and Tribal Communities in India: Role of Christian Organizations and Theological Education

BISHOP A.S. HEMROM

Introduction

In Indian situation 'religious sentiments' are the most highly inflammable elements which can be easily exploited for gains – be it commercial enterprises, political power struggles, socio-cultural movements or other like areas of concerns. Yes, if tactically and strategically dealt with, one may have the expected result very soon that too without much labour and pain. However, in 'secular' India that we live in, one somehow hesitates (even though it is done often) to openly play the game, but tries to employ some 'secular-type' of strategic means and methods to meet the expected end.

The Panos–Khonds episode or 'the riot' as it is called represents the same type of features. As I have gathered from different sources, the Kandhamal riot-2008 initially was not purely a religious problem; rather it had more the overtone of **economic reasons**. A couple of reasons attached to it were the issue of **Scheduled Tribe status** claimed by the Panos and the issue of **conversion** of Adivasis to Christianity. However, the case received a high tone of 'religious color' and impetus after the murder of Swami Lakshmanananda Saraswati (most likely owing to personal reasons). Even though the Maoist took the responsibility of killing the swami, the blame was put deliberately upon the Christian Panos. Perhaps, it provided strategically an 'opportunity-at-hand' with which the Hindu religious sentiments could be well exploited against the Panos, and it took the form of riot, killing a number of Christians and looting their belongings. Thanks to their sense of 'run-for-life' which drove many to hide in the jungles, or else many more would have been killed. It would have amounted to a sort of ethnic-cleansing of Christian Panos as well as Christian Khonds.

Our concern at this consultation of the Dalit-Adivasi interface is to reflect on the causes of the Kandhamal riot, its aftermath, and find out how we can bring peace. It is important to seek ways to establish and maintain peace, justice and reconciliation in this region – especially between the two warring ethnic communities... rather three communities. This Kandhamal episode very much includes and involves the local dominant Hindus who 'seem' to have played a major decisive role in the entire riot-episode. This paper seeks to identify and analyze vital reasons behind the riot and thereupon will come up with suggestions which might be helpful in our discussions aimed at finding possible solutions to the situation.

Moreover, Kandhamal episode is not a lone event which concerns or is restricted to the local Dalits and Advises of Kandhamal only. It very much represents and reflects on the exploitations and acts of oppressions being meted out against Advises and Dalits throughout India. Therefore, it is also necessary to refer the national scenario in this context, for, the case of Adivasis and Dalits is a collective social phenomenon. Whatever happens in a corner equally affects these communities in other parts of India. Likewise, any solution made to Adivasi-Dalit problems in a corner bears extensive and far-reaching implications for the whole ethnic communities in the country.

1.   Probable reasons behind Kandhamal Riot as we see it

As we have noted above, the basic reason for Kandhamal riot was not essentially 'religious' in its nature, but as it seems, the immediate cause was more that of economic nature. Gathered information reveals that the converted Panos were comparatively more educated and economically better off than the non-Christian Panos and the Khond Adivasis. Most of them had taken to small commercial activities in the form of shops and other enterprises constituting a sort of 'business community'. They were comparatively better off so much so that the local dominant Hindu-shopkeepers were facing difficulties in their business. They might have been jealous about the success of Panos, but could do nothing to bring them down. Some strategic means needed to be devised and designed. In this context, was the issue of Scheduled Tribe status as claimed by the Panos (before the government) brought to the fore to create rift between the Panos and the Kondhs? If ST status was given to Panos, they would have enjoyed and availed reservation provisions in employment- and again this could have brought more economic gain to the Panos further making them economically much more stronger and powerful. The dominant Hindu hardcore elements might have exaggerated the issue and instigated Khonds to confront the Panos. Would this have been the primary cause for the ethnic clash between both these communities? The third reason could have been the 'conversion' issue. However, this might not have generated more impetus and strength to create drift and clash between the two communities. However, the murder of the Swami seems to have provided an opportunity most favorable to promote the hate-campaign against Panos. Did they achieve this by exploiting the Hindu religious sentiments – prompted by a Hindu hidden-motive behind?

This paper will refer to some of the instances which in turn will reveal the various hidden motives of the dominant hardcore Hindu community and the dominant Indian community in general. This will enable us to understand their anti-Adivasi/Dalit Christian and also the anti-Adivasi/Dalit motives in general. Such instances can be traced almost everywhere with Dalits and Adivasis and mostly with those who have converted to Christianity. When we say 'dominant Hindu community' in relation to Adivasi-Dalit episode, it usually refers to a section of 'Indian community' (and not necessarily the Hindu religious community) - characterized with a specific exploitative Indian mind-set in general. This seems to be an innate mental property and an attitude dormant in individuals and represented in every area of life – be it political, economic, socio-cultural or the field of religion. Therefore, it is presumed that, a 'Hindu-conspiracy' cannot be fully ruled out in the Kandhamal riot episode. Hence, without giving any further reflection upon this 'conspiring mind-set' (– the probable cause behind the riot), we may not have any solution to Kandhamal problem. Kandhamal riot has been a representative case for all the problems the Indian Dalits and Adivasis face today. Moreover, the Kandhamal episode is not an isolated incident having 'occurred by chance', but is part of systematic plan in operation in India for a long time. Therefore, we presume that the 'dominant community' always has been a problem for Adivasi/Dalits, and they would remain so. One cannot expect good things to come to Adivasi-Dalits from such a community, and we speak this from our perception and experience from our day to day living. This implies that Adivasis and Dalits are to be prepared to write their own fate. It is with this pre-supposition that the paper will try to reflect and justify the opinion raised above.

2.   The Dominant Community's attitude towards Adivasis & Dalits

2.1. *The Preying Attitude*

Adivasis and Dalits from ages are being exploited by the dominant Indian communities in different ways and the very history witnesses to this fact. In every act of exploitation, the dominant Indian community in general is seen to have been motivated with a specific attitude of mind – which can best be identified to be the 'animal-like-attitude'. Seeing things from this perspective, one may conclude that we Indians do practice to live the philosophy of *'Jangal-raj'* - or the Darwinian philosophy of the 'survival of the fittest/mightiest'. The dominant/ mighty animals - the 'predators' in order to survive, generally depend upon the weaker animals which constitute their 'prey'. This implies that the dominants/mighty do have their survival only at the cost of the weaker animals. In our Indian social context, the same thing can be said. The Indian community- i.e. the 'Indian-human-kingdom' equally seems to have been practicing this 'jungle philosophy' and it is very much true when it concerns the Adivasis and Dalits –the weaker section of the Indian society. The Indian dominants cannot survive without exploiting the Adivasi and Dalits. Exploitation, as it seems, has become their 'biological- necessity' and this 'need' has helped them to develop their **'preying-attitude'which** makes them behave as if Adivasis and Dalits are non-human or sub-human entities. It is this attitude – a specific type of Indian mind-set (or Hindu mind-set) which defines the behaviours of the dominant community towards Adivasis and Dalits which can be seen in their strategic plans and programmes under the national policy planning in every sphere of life.

As for example the national development policy and its execution are very much indicative of this fact. It is in the name of 'national development' that millions of Adivasis and Dalits have been uprooted from their life-sustaining-resources by way of displacements. For, it is only after displacing them that the dominant community can have its foothold over those resources owned by Adivasis and Dalits. In the case of Jharkhand about 15 lacs people – mostly Adivasis and Dalits had been displaced between 1950 and 1995 just in the name of development. My question is: why does the government - represented by this dominant community choose to grab land (be it for mining, industry or construction of dams) mostly from the region largely populated by Adivasis and Dalits? Could it be the deliberate attempt/plotting on the part of the dominant community to efface the Adivasi-Dalit existence from their soil? Is it not equal to the act of preying?

2.2.   *Attitude of indifference towards Adivasi/Dalit cause*

The government budgetary plans earmark millions of rupees for the development and welfare programmes for Adivasis and Dalits, but development in these communities are hardly visible even after six decades of Indian independence. On the contrary, it is the dominant community which has benefited from such plans in various ways and forms. One can see an **'attitude of indifference'** or an **attitude of apathy** (or lack of motivation and will power as some say) in these people towards the development matters relating to Adivasis and Dalits.

This attitude of indifference/apathy presupposes an anti-Adivasi/Dalit mind-set which tends to say – 'let Adivasi/Dalits die by themselves', while keeping an eagle's eye/motive and waiting to feed on them and their belongings after they are dead. This is very much true and is measurable when one goes on to analyze the various developmental schemes implemented by the government agencies. Let us take for example one such case with the Jharkhand government. Due to the lack of motivation and will or the attitude of indifference towards the common people (mostly Adivasis and Dalits), the budgetary allotments relating to the areas of development and other welfare measures are not being properly and fully utilized. Crores of rupees are either misused or under-used and subsequently surrendered at the end of the fiscal year. Consequently, the ordinary down trodden people remain deprived of benefits while the dominant community gets the exploit. As for example, even though about 70-80% population depends upon agriculture, Jharkhand has only about 10-12% of its land with irrigation facilities in spite of the fact that plenty of schemes are in plan with major and minor irrigation provisions. Very recently, a local daily news paper in Ranchi came up with statistics which very much reflect the anti-Adivasi/Dalit attitude and apathy of the state government. The daily reports that, 19 mega irrigation projects which were started 40 years before are yet to be ready for operation (instead of the fact that, 3840 crores have been spent over against the initial budget of 446 crores). Had they been completed, the paper reports, 5.5 lac hectares of land would have been irrigated in Jharkhand (*Prabhat Khabar*, 15th Jan, 2011) and this would have been a boon for the farmers here. Unfortunately, between 60 and 70% of the rural population still lives below the poverty line. Besides, there are instances in which tones of food grains meant for distribution to the poor get rotted in the warehouses. Is it not the dominant community's apathy towards Adivasi/Dalits? These are but the few instances brought forth as examples.

3.   The Conspiracy of Invasion

Adivasis and Dalits have been the target of Hindu invasion since ages, and the nationwide history of these communities is very much indicative of this Hindu motive. There was a time when both these communities shared the same resources of the land, both being indigenous communities in India. Eventually the present Dalits were invaded, subjugated and enslaved for perpetual exploitation. The present Adivasis, the freedom-loving communities, generally escaped and moved to other regions. Thus for a long time they enjoyed the freedom from any form of alien interference, maintaining their specific socio-cultural identity and geographical enclaves. However, now it is unfortunate that they too are facing and sharing almost the same fate of Dalits today. A constant process of *'Dalitization of Adivasis'* is carried over by the dominant community with well devised plans and programmes with tactical means and strategies which can be seen in different forms as explained below.

3.1. *'Development' as a means to make inroads to Adivasi/Dalit world*

Till 1970s the 5th Scheduled areas were kept within the provision of 'partial exclusion' with a view to restrict the alien intrusion and thereby provided protection to the Adivasi interest. However, in the name of 'promoting' the developmental activities (for Adivasis and the nation) the provision was lifted giving free passage to non-Tribals. The fifth schedule also restricted purchase of land for building of private houses by the 'development officials' from Adivasis. Fortunately, this restriction of transfer of land by Adivasis to the non-Adivasis is still in force although it is deliberately and largely being violated. Besides, Adivasi land is being illegally and forcibly taken away by the intruders, and this happens in spite of the fact that the fifth Schedule guarantees the 'inalienability' of Adivasi land. In the case of Jharkhand Adivasis, the land is legally protected under the two Acts – the Chotanagpur Tenancy Act, 1908 and the Santhal Pargana Tenancy Act. Today the fact remains, that we, the Adivasi and Dalits do perceive the pain and suffering of the 'internal-colonization' (as some call it) of our fate. A time will come, when we would be finally driven out of our ancestral land. There was a time when our forefathers escaped farther into the interior forest whenever there was alien intrusion, but as the signs show, we do not have place to escape any more. Time is coming when Adivasis will be finally 'domesticated' and enslaved ... and this will be the final invasion of the Adivasi world. Again a Dalit community will be created out of the indigenous population.

Yes, it is very likely that the political phase of the 'internal colonization' of 'Adivasi Jharkhand' will be fully materialized in near future. In the present political scenario the Adivasis are simply seen and used as 'voting-tools' and nothing more than that. All the spheres of the political Jharkhand – it's power, authority and various government agencies,as well as the resources - have already been 'captured' by the 'dominant bureaucracy' – identified to be the *Jhas,*

Mishras and *Pandeys* etc. This is one reason why people have started calling it to be the *"Jha-Khand"* or the second Bihar instead of Jharkhand.

3.2.   *The Culture as means for the ideological invasion*

Prompted by the hidden agenda of colonization ("Integrating the Tribal people into the main stream Hindu order" in the words of Balasaheb Deshpande, *Sunday*,31st October,1998), the Hindutva elements consciously are trying to make inroads into the Adivasi world, and it is the culture which proves to be the more effective means. This plan involves the agenda of 'Hinduization' of the Adivasi world, and different strategies have been devised for this and effectively employed since a long time. Consequently, baring the Christian community (about 10-12% of Adivasi population of Jharkhand) and the few Sarnites (the followers of traditional Adivasi religion), the large part of Adivasis have been Hinduised from the religious point of few. The census of Bihar1981, reported 80% Adivasis to be Hindus. This they could achieve by consciously promoting the Hindu rituals like holding of *yangyas*, recitation of popular literature *Ram Charitmanasa*, festivals like Ramnavami, Deewali, Raksha Bandhan, Rath yatra etc. into the Adivasi world under the banner of Vanvasi Kalyan Ashram/VKS (1952). VKS, later renamed as Akhil Bhartiya Vanvasi Kalyan Ashram/ABVKA (during emergency), a sister organization of RSS had a mandate to penetrate into 276 tribal dominated districts of the country. Till October, 1998 the organization had a sway over 20,000 tribal villages with its various programs (600 centers, 107 students' hostel, 399 medical centers and 1,197 schools managed by 1,100 fulltime workers, *Sunday*, 31st Oct, 1998)

At present special emphasis is being made to have inroads into the Adivasi world of Jharkhand, and they have decided to go the Christian Missionaries' way. The DAV group has been assigned with this task. Nirmal Kumar Singh, the organizer-cum the Coordinator of the DAV foundation, in one of the meetings held in Ranchi in 2006 stated "To spread its influence the churches have picked on health, education and socio-economic development. This has gained them quick inroads into the tribal societies. We have also decided to follow this" [*Indian Telegraph*, (Ranchi edn.), 9th January, 2006]. The foundation started with schools initially with five Blocks of Khunti district, having plan to carry out in all the 222 Development Blocks in the state of Jharkhand.

Vidya Bharti, another sister organization of RSS, has already established its aim – (according to Dr. Ashok Vaisneya, the RSS state Pracharak for Jharkhand), which seeks 'to reach out to the society through children' (Prahbat *Khabar*, 4.2.2002), of course in the name of building the Adivasi society through the means of 'education' under the scheme of 'Saraswati Shishu Mandir'!. According to Vananchal Siksha Samiti, which manages the programs, already 152 Development Blocks, out of 222, have been covered with this scheme till the reporting time. Whatever claim is made about the aim of these enterprises, the hidden agenda is to mould the tender minds of children into the Hindu mind-set and ideology completing the invasion of Adivasi and Dalit world.

Apart from what have been said above, there are many other programmes and strategies which aim at pushing through the hidden agenda which seeks to establish a sort of religious imperialism in India to be ruled over by the philosophy/ideology of Hindutva – which seeks to build up a *Ram Raj*- implying a Hindu Rashtra, and not the Kingdom of Ram (implying god) as envisaged by Mahatma Gandhi.

4.   Healing and Restoration: The probable ways and means
The problem is of perennial nature and it has been made so due to the involvement of 'third party' – we have identified it in the form of Hidutva elements, and therefore, the solution to the problem does not seem to be that easy to propose due to the following reasons:.

a)   If you ask the converted Panos to be reconverted to their old faith (apparently Hindu in this context) – which is demanded of them by the Kondhs or the Hindutva elements, they would not be doing so. For, having tasted the state of enlightenment, sense of freedom, and joy of life by embracing Christian faith, they will not go back to the old faith and tradition. They find Hinduism to be something that had been exploiting them in different ways for ages. The faith and tradition, which they once belonged to, never gave them a respectable identity and social status in the mainstream Indian society. They would never like to go back again to the world of darkness.

b)   As long as the Panos remain Christians, the rift may/will remain forever between them and the Kondhs, because of the 'third party element' involved in the episode.

c)   As long as the Kondhs keep identifying themselves to be 'Hindus' (who are essentially not), the problem may remain the same due to their religious affinity with the third party elements.

d)   The Hindutva elements represented by the local dominant community may not be willing to make 'compromises' in their policy of subjugation and exploitation of the Dalits and Adivasis. Moreover, there is the 'economic interest' on the part of the local dominant business community and so of the powerful corporate world dominated by the dominant section of Indian society, which at the same time enjoys the political patronage both at the local and national level.

e)   What is more critical is, as long as the economic imbalance and unequal social status remain between Panos and the Kondhs, the social environment will remain charged with the feeling of jealousy and hatred for one another. Besides, as long as Dalits and Adivasis remain uneducated, poor and marginalized, the 'dominance' of the third-party-elements would always be there disturbing the probable peaceful co-existence between two ethnic communities.

All the above points suggest the need to have strong steps to bring about healing and reconciliation. A **case study** may help us find the solution here.

A Case Study: Kandhamal episode of Jharkhand –

In the month of October, 2008 a tense atmosphere had built up between the Christian Adivasis and the non-Christian Adivasis following the issue of translation of the Bible into local Kurukh/ Oraon language. In the process of translation few words used in some passages did hurt the sentiment of the non-Christian Adivasis, and they took up the case and made a 'communal' issue out of it. This episode is known to be the infamous "Nemha Bible" episode.

The incident would not have been that inflammatory had the Hindutva elements not instigated the non-Christian Adivasis. There were plans and strategies devised to create a 'Kandhamal-like-episode' out of this event. The non-Christian Adivasis, who have affinity with the Hindutva elements (– simply because they are not Christians), were about to launch a riot-like situation. However, this did not happen, thanks for the divine intervention. It was a section of the non-Christian Adivasis who came forward to defuse this prevailing unprecedented 'Intra-Adivasi/Tribal ethnic conflict'. After two years by now, the issue still remains alive and lingering, however, in an inactive way with cases pending in the court of justice.

If one analyzes this episode, the Bible translation was not the sole reason for this. It was translated years ago, and had invited no reaction of any form whatsoever so far. Somehow, in the process of looking for issues to be 'politicized' against Christian Adivasis (just in the wake of or coinciding Kandhamal event); this matter seems to have been brought to the fore all of a sudden unexpectedly by the Hindutva elements. Actually, since long non-Christian Adivasis have been made prey to the conspiracy of the Hindu fundamentalists, and there have been deliberate constant efforts to turn non-Christian Adivasis against Christian. The over-all motive behind this has been to 'divide and weaken' the tribal unity and solidarity, and thereby to subjugate and colonize them so as to facilitate the exploitation of Adivasis and the rich resources that they have. In this process the Hindutva elements always wanted to create hatred towards Christians by way of promoting a sense of jealousy based on the fact that Christians are comparatively better off and established. Further, it is because of this Christian community that the Hindutva elements are not fully successful in fulfilling their **"mission-invasion"**. Finally, the non-issue was made a burning issue just by exploiting the 'religious sentiments' of the non-Christian Adivasis. The situation, however, keeps cool at present.

An analysis: How the intra-Adivasi conflict calmed down and Church failed?

By the time church leaders were planning to deal with the event, a section of non-Christian Adivasi community, who literally adhere to the traditional religion called *Sarna*, met the church leaders. These were the leaders who were quite educated and enlightened, well informed about the hidden and exploitative agenda of the Hindutva elements. They were quite aware of the fact that the Hindutva elements wanted to create rift and enmity between both groups to gain their own interest. The pro-Christian Adivasis stood up with church, and things calmed down. At the first sight, the solution looked too easy?

Church 'interpreted' the episode to be a 'divine intervention'. This is because, since long the churches in Jharkhand had the unsuccessful attempts to come together with non-Christian Adivasis for dialogue to create an atmosphere for peaceful co-existence and common efforts for the development of the Adivasi community. But, this opportunity came to them by-chance in the guise of *Nemha Bible* episode. This failure, which the church had earlier in this context, was due to church's apathy for and towards the non-Christian Adivasis. Actually church had 'distanced' itself from them just because of the fact that – Christians, after adhering to Christian faith became the 'civilized' section of the Adivasi population, and therefore had to maintain a considerable "distance" from the 'uncivilized' Adivasis as such, and so from the many traditions and cultural elements – which the church then termed to be *"Sansarik"* meaning the worldly or profane. This situation created a sense of bitterness in the non-Christian Adivasi community against Christians. Taking this opportunity, the Hindutva elements made an easy inroad in to the non-Christian Adivasi world and have strong hold over them and have been using this section of community for its own end.

The church again failed to make use of this 'God-given-opportunity', and gradually losing the support of the section of non-Christians which came to the aid of the church at this critical moment. Actually by making use of the opportunity, the church could form one forum in the name of Adivasi Mahasabha (a sort of Confederation) and jointly had started addressing Adivasi issues and challenges.

However, in the process of moving together, the Sarna faction did put forth some (not-very-difficult & impracticable) 'demands' (which could have benefited in the area of education of their children apart from other things) from the 'elder brothers'. Unfortunately, the church seems to have failed to give 'respect' to the demands. This prompted non-Christian counterpart to distance from this forum. The forum/Adivasi Mahasabha, however, still operates with few members. Regrettably, I myself am one of the core members in the central executive of this forum!

5.   Theological implications of Kandhamal riot and church's role towards peace-building

During the time when I was doing my BD studies, I was deliberately building myself with the literature pertaining to liberation theology. Somehow, it is during this time that, I came across some books (which were gifted to me by one American professor) like *Politics of Jesus, Economy of the Gospel and The Original Revolution*. The book 'Economy of the Gospel' came up with a statement which said, the enslavement of the 'Blacks' is the out come of Noah's curse made over Ham- the second son of Noah, who represents the people with black complexion (while Shem represents white and Japheth (Yepet) represents the people with yellow complexion), I was literally struck by this statement. It was a curse of Noah given to Ham who dared to see the naked body of his father that his descendants would be made enslaved by the descendants of Shem and Yepet. The writer, further went on to justify that, the blacks of Africa and Asia in the tropical region do belong to the offspring of Ham, and therefore have been enslaved by either whites or yellows for ages and to the present.

I wonder if the story has some potential truth. I cannot say if the curse of Noah still binds upon the children of Ham? But then, it is a vital theological question that we need to reflect upon. Could it be a part of the divine economy or providence? If not, is there at least some reality? Are the blacks made for exploitation by the whites or the yellows –as the human history witnesses for ages so far? If not, why have the Adivasis and Dalits been suffering from ages at the hands of the yellow Aryans? Is not this exploitation of a perennial nature? Are

Adivasis and Dalits made to serve the Aryan interest? No particular answer is thinkable of the questions raised.

Under the philosophy of *'Jungle raj'*, I see lions and tigers to be the predators which feed on the weaker animals. Can ever, the weaker animals be made free, saved and secured from the predators? In the jungle raj of 'Human kingdom' in India, I see and experience the Aryans – symbolized to be exploiters who have been feeding on at the cost of the marginalized – the Adivasis and Dalits. Can we ever be free from the clutch of the invading Aryans?

I have no intention to dampen the spirit of anyone by raising unnecessary questions, but then wanted to convey that it is not easy to deal with these questions. It needs and demands intensive thinking, planning and strategizing on our part. Liberation theology derives its inspiration from Christ the liberator, who is still engaged in the liberative task of the poor, oppressed and exploited, and that He has entrusted this task to the church – his bride. Since its inception, the church has been doing this successfully, and we can also do it provided we consider some of the following points. I hope that the following questions will provide us with some theological insights which will help us deal with the problem theologically:

a)   So far we have been blaming the Hidutva elements in RSS for whatever happened in Kandhamal. Should the church not bear any responsibility and blame itself for what happened in Kandhamal?

b)   Churches have been serving for the over-all development of its 'own sheep', ignoring the 'sheep-outside-the fold'. Is the church not responsible in creating a sense of hatred, jealousy and thereby bitterness in the minds of the non-Christian Adivasis and Dalits in the region? Is it not the church which is responsible for 'distancing' Christian Panos from the Kondhs who had peacefully co-existed since ages?

c)   We blame RSS elements for 'instigating' non-Christians against Christians. Why did the church not take any initiative to educate, inform and empower at least a small section of the non-Christian ethnic community - the Kondhs, who could have stood by the side of the church at that critical moment?

d)   Does the church in Kandhamal or in Odisha acknowledge and repent for its miss-takes, and be prepared to rethink and re-strategize its ministry?

e)   Why is it that the church does not include the 'dominant community' within the purview of its ministry? Is it not true that Christ died for them too?

Conclusion

In my opinion, the church has to plan for a specific **'Kondh-mission'**. Of course, it should probably not under the banner of the 'Church' – as the word has assumed 'allergic-potentials' not acceptable to the non-Christian Kondhs and the dominant community around. The church may work through or depute non-Christian social workers and peace-makers armed with 'Christian spirituality' and commitment, who would initiate a development process involving every section of the society and social awareness for a peaceful co-existence.

In order to move on with 'Kondh-Mission', we as church need to be prepared for certain compromises and sacrifices. Can we not adopt strategies like St. Paul did? He, in order to achieve his mission became Jew for Jews, Roman for Romans and Gentile for Gentiles. Can we sacrifice some of the church/ faith elements that restrict us from going to the Kondhs?

Jesus advised his disciples to behave differently at times like doves or snakes. Can we not be that tactical in our mission-approach?

Finally, I would say the predators always feed on the weaker animals, but then if the people-under prey are made enlightened and empowered (at least some section of the community) in real sense of the term, it is likely that a balanced and peaceful atmosphere could be built in to live with. Moreover in Indian situation it is money that vindicates. Of course, simultaneously the church has to preach the gospel of *'metanoia'*- implying change of mind-set and attitude to the Brahmins and the rich.

Money matters, and plays important and vital role as it leads and helps one to live a life with all its 'abundance'. Jesus came with the clear aim - to give 'life-in all its-abundance' preferably to the poor and the marginalized, and in this way tried to bring and provide social justice to them - a social status and dignity to be respected and reckoned with in the larger society which would help maintain a balance in social co-existence. Jesus, in this process had envisioned to create a situation marked with peace, prosperity and stability - a *'shalomic situation'* symbolized in the Kingdom of God on earth. Will the Church, which has been so far working for the 'eternal life up in the heaven' also start working for a 'heaven on earth'? We presume, in this process a new-heaven-like -situation can be created in Kandhamal in which the 'preying lions' will no more bring any harm to the weaker animals, but will satisfy themselves by grazing grass.

Media Reflection on Kandhamal

MR DIBIN SAMUEL

I wouldn't want to take a lot of time, but just like to add few lines, sharing my experience working in the stream of Christian journalism, and how particularly the 2008 mayhem in Kandhamal had changed and challenged my life to a great extent.

I should confess here that nothing has truly stirred and awakened me like Kandhamal of the many themes and incidents I have written about. In fact it was a very mundane thing at the beginning, just write and interpret the various programs and initiatives of the church which I should admit was very cushy and convenient. But that ruinous attack and persecution of Christians in Kandhamal led me to ask a lot of questions on my work, life and even my personal faith. The stories of people being brutally killed, their houses burnt and the forceful migration of hundreds of thousands started to deeply pain me and challenged my identity as a media person and also as a Christian.

It really made me come out of my cocoon and see a different world out there. In fact the most inspiring of the lot was that the people, in spite of the persecution, pain, hunger and homelessness, holding on to their faith and asserting that nothing is more important than Christ. I am not sure if we as people working in faith organisations would make such a declaration after losing everything and being forced into some jungle. So whether I am a journalist, reverend or activist, we all have the same obligation of voicing and working for the poor and weak. In fact the realisation of the importance of my position and responsibility in the wake of such unprecedented violence against Christians, sparked in me a great interest to do what I do...with love and total commitment.

I remember a Reverend who during a recent Dalit conference said "God is never neutral and takes sides in the context of oppression. God stands with the lowly against lofty and manifests his glory through the oppressed." I think if as Church we don't stand for the oppressed and fight for them, we stand for none. Christ stands on their side, and when we realise that and become aware of our identity, that is when we start to genuinely be concerned and use our position and resources efficiently.

Now talking about the role of media, without me mentioning you all know how biased and unfair they were. In fact many media outlets were manipulated by powers and for months kept repeating on normalcy being restored while people were still homeless and without any adequate support for their daily living. Even the figures that they published on the number of deaths, the number of homeless and those injured, were irrefutably false. Surprisingly, despite the violence being large-scale many newspapers still placed the news on the third or fourth page. Besides that, the cases and the judgements that followed also were rarely highlighted.

Without question, media has a role in framing, shaping and promoting public opinion to ensure people make responsible and informed choices than out of ignorance and misinformation. It can play both a negative and constructive role in either fuelling conflict or preventing conflict or contributing to peace building efforts. Sadly post-Kandhamal news, especially the vernacular media deliberately created misrepresentations in reporting and indulged in spreading propaganda against Christians which only caused more hate and divide. Unfortunately, the significant sections of the media houses were co-opted by the riot organizers and merely acted as propaganda mouthpieces. But thanks to many Christian activists and watchdogs who voiced for the suffering and intensified the issue so the accused would be put behind bars and justice would be brought to the victims.

We have seen how - erroneous communication - and misinformation were used to instigate mobs and cause great mayhem. More conflicts would be seen if we fail to see the need for church to contribute for better communication and networking.

There is an urgent need to address the much vulnerability that undermines the positive role media could play in peace building in post-Kandhamal.

We can't entirely put the burden on the outside media, but as church must encourage and train our people to play a crucial role by introducing Christian values for ethical communication and for forming a just society.

The Church needs to increase her presence in the world of Mass Media in order to communicate the social and moral teachings of the Gospel.

Church must use journalism to educate people on social justice, civil liberties and human dignity.

Church must also strongly consider establishing contacts with civil bodies and secular media people which will be of great help in the longer run.

We also need more people from the Christian community who can write thought-provoking features and editorials on social, political, religious and moral issues.

It is high time Church invests more personnel and finances in the work of communications for the years to come.

Thank You!

Dalit and Tribal Women – Instruments of Peace and Reconciliation amidst Violence

-MS.MASOPHY KENGOO

Introduction

I come from a small village from the hills of Manipur State, which is also known as the Kohinoor of India belonging to a Naga tribe. Coming from a state where internal division within indigenous population has surfaces as the main cause of strife in the State and also where tribalism/communalism is prevalent and insurgency is highest in the country, life has not been easy for us even from our childhood days. I still remember vividly the incident that happened when I was in standard VIII. Once we went to our mother's village for a Golden Jubilee Celebration of Christianity in that village. The night before the celebration the village was attacked by underground insurgents of another tribal group killing many people. The memories are still fresh in my mind; I can still hear the sound of the guns, the shouting and the cries of the women and the children; and the sight of the dead bodies. This is the kind of life that majority of the people experience from their childhood.

Insurgency and Armed Forces Special Power Act (AFSPA)

The AFSPA was passed by the Government of India in 1958 by an act of Parliament. Under this Act the Security Forces were given the license to shoot to kill. They can 'fire on' or otherwise use force, even cause death, to any person on even a sheer reason of suspicion. It allows the Forces to make an arrest without a warrant and can enter and search any premise to make arrests. Under this Act, all security forces are given unrestricted and unaccounted power to carry out their operations, once an area is declared disturbed.

Manipur has the highest number of insurgent groups in the country. They have their own demands and political ideologies but most importantly all these insurgency is related to the AFSPA. Thousands of innocent lives were lost under this Act. The Security Forces has so much of power with this Act that they can and will stop the young people who are mostly college students and do their body and identity check. They will even check how much money they are carrying in their wallet and will take away some of their cash and if they report back, they have all the power if they want, to even kill the person, giving them the tag of being an insurgent. The young people are helpless and can do nothing. For this reason my mother never allows my brothers to go to Imphal without me or my mother accompanying them. For every little thing we have to accompany them. If a mother or sister accompanies them they don't stop the young people and I will have a right to challenge them. Hence, I realize and come to the conclusion that indeed women have a role to bring peace and reconciliation in this troubled land.

Women's role in Peace Healing and Reconciliation

In Manipur there is a women's group called the Meira Paibis (Torch Bearers). At the local level these women have been playing a significant role in peace building through mediating between warring factions demanding justice and repeal of emergency laws (AFSPA); and building community wide support for peace and reconciliation. Whenever incidents of violence happen, all the women will come out bearing the torch whether it is day or night and they will wrestle till peace is restored. In every house where there is a woman there will be a torch. The Meira Paibis vaulted into the International media's eyes following their naked protest against the outrage of likely rape, torture and killing of Ms. Manorama by paramilitary forces. An innovative approach in mediating between warring parties and in mediating peace for peace and reconciliation across political divides has been demonstrated also by the Naga women. Some 3000 mothers from different Naga tribes launched the 'Shed no more Blood' campaign under the banner of the

Naga Mothers Association (NMA). NMA and the Naga Women's Movement of Manipur (NWUM) have worked together both with the underground Armed Leaders and the security forces to mobilize communities for reconciliation; sustaining the ceasefire and promoting an inclusive peace process. As interlocutors and facilitators, they have traversed conflict lines and fighting faction, and encouraged the participation of different tribes and neighboring states and communities in the non violent peace effort.

Apart from these local women groups the best example would be of Ms. Irom Sharmila who is known as the Iron Lady of Manipur. She is continuing her fast unto death hunger strike for the tenth year demanding the repeal of the draconian law, The Arm Forces Special Power Act of the Indian Government. It all started on the fated day of Thursday, November 2, 2000, when the notorious Assam Rifles indiscriminately and without provocation gunned down a group of 10 citizens at a bus stop in Malom in retaliation to an alleged attack on their convoy the same morning by unknown persons. Most of those killed were women and children. Irom Sharmila Chanu, who was then a 28-year-old young human rights activist, went up to her mother Sukhi Devi, sought her blessings and quickly decided to prolong her weekly Thursday fast. Thus came the beginning of the legendary fast-unto-death of an ordinary, young, almost an apolitical Manipuri woman, who, until now, would ride on bicycle to the meetings and the markets, living a quiet and obscure life.

Her determination, her resolve, is a negation of the brutality of the establishment and an affirmation of the positive dimensions of resistance, the will to fight and hope for a better world, without violence and injustice. People like Sharmila, and the mothers and women of Manipur have become the face and perhaps the solution for an unceasing war.

Conclusion

As we go back to the pages of history, one thing we can notice is that whenever there is any sort of conflict or tension in any part of the world the women and the children are the worst affected group or in other words they are always at the receiving end. However, despite being afflicted, harassed; and life being at its worst the women have come up with great courage and sincere love for their people and as such they stand up for the rights of the people. And above all, they strive to bring about cordial relationship between the two warring parties so as to enable the fellow citizens to live in peace and harmony.

The context of Manipur and Kandhamal is similar even though the violence in Kandhamal is more to do with religious fundamentalism. However, in both cases it is the women who suffer the most. Like the women of the troubled state of Manipur and other North Eastern states the Women of Orissa especially from Kandhamal have a big role to play in bringing peace. I am not saying that they should do what the Manipuri women are doing but I am just citing an example. They can be agents of peace in a very different way but their motivation should be to end the violent conflicts and to help people and families overcome the emerging economic and social problems resulting from the conflicts. What needs to be done is to equip themselves as peace builders and to stop their children from harboring feelings of revenge. Women have the opportunity to do this as they interact more with their children. Women should also actively participate in the promotion of peace education and other peace related activities by organizing and participating in peace marches, seminars, workshops, training events and informal discussions. Way to socializing and interfaith dialogue should also start from the family level where values are taught. The family unit is the place where peaceful spirit is planted and positive outlooks can be developed. Just as a mother stops a fight between siblings within the four corners of her house, a woman can always be an important instrument in stopping a fight among her neighbours. She can extend this role to stop violence at national and international levels too.

Every woman encounters a situation of violence and faces the aftermath; but Dalit and Tribals women are most affected by the violent situations. They are doubly affected as their community is already being discriminated within the Indian society apart from their status being women. In such situations they just don't have to wait, watch and expect other women's organizations or NGO's to come and help them but take up their responsibilities and understand their unique position to resist, fight and champion their cause as the ones who can bring peace and harmony to the society.

Dalit Tribal Interface: Healing and Restoration

DEAN NATHANIEL BM

Introduction and Greetings

As we've been talking about 'the causes and aftermath of the Kandhamal Riots which occurred in 2008 and efforts towards peace, Justice and Reconciliation', I would like to throw some light on some of the issues. My hearty thanks goes to Dr. Hrangthan Chhungi (Executive Secretary Commission on Tribal & Adivasi, National Council of Churches in India) for giving me this opportunity and Bishop P. K. Samantaroy (Bishop Diocese of Amritsar, Church of North India) for encouraging me to present my views on the issue. Before I say anything I would like to read out a poem from the Gitanjali written by great writer Rabindranath Tagore where he wants his country to be a country of peace and harmony.

"Where the mind is without fear and the head is held high;
Where knowledge is free;
Where the world has not been broken up
into fragments by narrow domestic walls;
Where words come out from the depth of truth;
Where tireless striving stretches its arms towards perfection;
Where the clear stream of reason
has not lost its way into the dreary desert sand of dead habit;
Where the mind is led forward by thee into ever-widening
thought and action—
Into that heaven of freedom, my Father, let my country
awake."

India is a country with many colours. Though India is multilingual, multicultural and a multi religious/faith society, yet the people of India are known for their love and hospitality. They know how to cope with others; they know how to live with strangers. At the grass-root level the people of India live in peace and harmony with each other. They greet each other with love and respect, no matter which religion they belong to. If we want to witness this love we should then have a glimpse of any Indian festivals where we find Hindus greeting Muslim friends on *Eid* and Muslims greeting Hindu friends on *Diwali*. I remember my friend from Australia saying "if we have this many differences in our country we will surely kill each other". India has set an example of communal harmony to the whole world.

On the darker side, India has witnessed communal riots almost every year after independence. No year in India has been riot-free. Some years are particularly noticeable like 1992-93 when post Babri Masjid demolition violence occurred, in 2002 Gujarat witnessed major communal disaster, and again in 2008 Kandhamal riots and in many years there were riots which are not nationally taken notice of. The year 2010 of course did not witness riots like Mumbai in 1992-93 or one like in Gujarat in 2002 but did witness riots mostly in either middle level cities or even small towns and villages.[1]

We hoped that the year 2008 may be a riot-free year for the first time in 60 years after independence. However, soon this hope was belied and riots began to take place like every year. Though again most of the riots were not major, towards the end of the year even that hope was belied. As usual police behaviour was totally partial though with few exceptions and minorities received the drubbing.

Another peculiarity of 2008 was major communal violence against Christians for the first time in post-independent India. Although Christians have been under attack for several years it was doubtful and not very distinct until 2008 where we witnessed a major communal violence against Christian minority in Kandhamal district of Orissa. The Sangh Parivar was never in such foul mood against this tiny

---

[1] *http://www.en.wikipedia.org/wiki/Religious_violence_in_orissa* Dated. 03-01-2011

minority which has rendered great services in the field of education and health. Terrible violence against Christians in Kandhamal district was witnessed on 1st January 2008; in fact, riots against Christians had already erupted on 25th December 2007 during Christmas celebration in different places in Kandhamal. Several houses belonging to Christians were burnt in the villages of Sripala, Rebingia, Nuapadar and Kasinapadar in Kandhamal district. Some 10 houses were set ablaze in these villages. During these incidents several people fled to jungles or to other villages.

It would be interesting to mention here that former chief Justice of India Justice V.N. Khare on 19th January 2008 called for setting up of an autonomous body to deal with communal riots cases stating that it is the state *rajdharma* (duty) to protect the minorities. Justice Khare said that communal riots should not be treated merely as law and order problem. He said that such riots are a serious problem and a serious view of the matter should be taken. Justice Khare also demanded that a special law be enacted to promote safety for minorities. He also observed "Where is the right to life if minorities are victimized and those who victimize are not prosecuted and instead go scot free?"[2]

But who would listen to this voice of sanity and year after year minorities suffer in these riots and rioters indeed go off the hook. The Federal Government could not even enact the Communal Riots Bill for which it had given solemn promise. It is still gathering dust and now there will be hardly any Parliament session to take it up before next elections take place and the Bill will naturally expire. So, this is the concern of the secular government that its priorities are hardly serious to prevent communal violence!

Can the Kandhamal Riots of 2008 be referred to as a 'mishap in the region and between the two religions'? Shri Manmohan Singh, the prime minister of India calls them a 'shame'. They just did not ignite the religious sentiments of people in the Kandhamal region but left us all in utter shock. Three years back when I was doing my theological studies in Pune, and when these riots were going on, we used to sit and gaze at the newspaper and discuss the breakdown in the region,

---

[2] *Ibid.*

where people were blaming each other and disrupting the peace there. It was definitely an act of humiliation for the entire country.

I remember in the month of November 2010, NCCI-Commission on youth organized an interfaith conference on peace-future, and in the group discussion with people representing different faiths, there was a strong suggestion to work on the problems due to conversions, especially as they trigger violence in the country. It is to be noted here, that forced conversions do not take place everywhere and if they do happen are very sporadic instances. The sad part is- there is nothing firm that has come out to help us in this thing.

The constitution of India in its Preamble describes India as a secular state but such incidents which tarnish the secular fabric of the country actually leave us dump founded. The Constitution of India declares the nation to be a "secular republic that must uphold the right of citizens to freely worship and propagate any religion or faith (with activities subject to reasonable restrictions for the sake of morality, law and order, etc.)".[3] The Constitution of India also declares the right to freedom of religion as a fundamental right. The word 'secular' in the constitution was included by the forty second amendment act, 1976. The state has no official religion. Secularism pervades its provisions which give full opportunity to all persons to profess, practice and propagate religion of their choice. The constitution not only guarantees a person's freedom of religion and conscience, and thoroughly restrains the state from making any discrimination on grounds of religion. It is generally perceived that the causes of religious conflicts are political rather than ideological in nature.[4]

Issues behind the Conflict in the Area

Behind the clashes are long-simmering tensions between equally impoverished groups: the Khandas (Kondhs) constitute around 80% of the population of the people residing in the region and the Panas (Panos - Dalit Christians) the non-tribal people, constitute the second largest population of the people. Both are original inhabitants of the

---

[3] *http://www.en.wikipedia.org/wiki/Religion_in_india* Dated. 05-01-2011.
[4] *Ibid.*

land. The Indian tradition of 'untouchability', where Dalits, the so-called out caste' people, are subject to social and economic discrimination is outlawed in the Indian constitution. The prejudices remain and 'conversion' out of 'untouchability' has been a push factor for millions of such people to escape from their circumstances through joining other religions. The Panas have converted to Christianity in large numbers and prospered financially.[5] Over the past several decades, most of the Panas have become Dalit Christians. The Kandhamal Riots, as we know, were a result of the conflict between people of 'Khand tribe' and the panas (Dalit Christians). The way it's been reflected, the 'Conspiracy' behind it is concealed from us. Orissa's new Director General of Police Manmohan Praharaj said a conspiracy had been hatched to kill Swami. Ashok Sahu, President of Hindu Jagaran Samukhya, alleges, "Swami was killed as per a meticulously thought out plan."

Brannon Parker in his book "Orissa in the Crossfire" provides many vital details related to the Hindu-Christian violence that has swept Orissa's Kandhamal district. The eye-opening book also highlights the history of Orissa and its tribes. While many have familiarized themselves with the propaganda that has fictionalized the events surrounding the Kandhamal crisis, few have had access to the facts.

The true history of Kandhamal and the struggles of its people deserve a fair hearing in the court of public opinion. Is the Kandha religion sinister or sacred? Are they bloodthirsty savages or a people of a noble and ancient heritage? Can the Tribals of Kandhamal rise up out of their undeserved shame and be seen for who they really are? Long labeled as 'a cruel human sacrificing tribe of ruthless savages' it is time the truth be revealed. It is time for the world to learn about the Kandha 'God of Light' and their Culture of Life rather than simply criticizing them. So here I wanted to say that we should not blame the Khandas and Panas for the riots but we must condemn the conspiracy behind the conflict which reminds me the British policy "Divide and

---

[5] *http://www.en.wikipedia.org/wiki/Religious_violence_in_orissa* Dated. 06-01-2011.

rule". That is what has happened in Kandhamal where Dalits and Tribals have been suffering and politicians enjoying the play.[6]

Conversion Controversy

Hindu nationalist groups have blamed the violence on the issue of religious conversion. Conversions have been legislated by the provisions of the Freedom of Religion Acts, replicated in some of the states in India. Orissa was the first state of independent India to enact legislation on religious conversions. The Orissa Freedom of Religion Act, 1967, stipulates that no person shall "convert or attempt to convert, either directly or otherwise, any person from one religious faith to another by the use of force or by inducement or by any fraudulent means".[7] Hindus claim that the Christian missionaries were converting poor tribal people by feeding them with beef, which is taboo in Hinduism. Also, the missionaries would upgrade the mud houses of the converts into brick-lime. Hindus have further alleged that the increase in the number of Christians in Orissa has been a result of exploitation of illiteracy and impoverishment by the missionaries. The Census of India shows that Christian population in Kandhamal grew from around 43,000 in 1981 to 117,950 in 2001. Conversion from Hinduism is frowned upon by right-wing parties such as the Vishwa Hindu Parishath. Conversion has been a major factor behind the riots because some of the Hindu fundamentalists couldn't tolerate the Christian growth in the region. Justice S C Mohapatra, heading the one-man panel, said in his interim report on the violence in Kandhamal which claimed 43 lives besides damaging many houses and churches says, "Sources of the violence were deeply rooted in land disputes, conversion and re-conversion and fake certificate issues,"[8] If forcible conversion is a reality then why is Christianity even today a minority religion in India, more so when the Faith came to India 2000 years back?

---

[6] Telephonic Interview with Haramani Digal, B.D 3rd. Student, Bishop's College Kolkata(Resident of Kandhamal Dist. Orissa), Dated. 09-01-2011.

[7] http://www.en.wikipedia.org/wiki/Religious_violence_in_orissa Dated. 06-01-2011.

[8] http://www.indiatimes.com Dated. 07-01-2011.

Reservation

As I have mentioned earlier over the years the Panas due to poverty and ignorance have been converted to Christianity and some of their leaders today are retired IAS, IPS, OAS officers and owners of NGOs. According to reservation rules even though the Scheduled Tribes continue to enjoy the benefits of reservation after conversion to other religions but Hindu Scheduled Castes after conversion cease to belong to any caste, hence legally treated as general category. The converted Panas now want to enjoy the benefits of reservation by circumventing the current rules. To do that, their leaders, one of whom is a Member of Parliament from Congress Party, by putting pressure on the congress government at the centre has successfully included the nomenclature of their language (Kui) which is originally the dialect of the Kandha (STs) of that area, in the central list of reserved categories. The Constitution of the country categorically refuses reservation on linguistic lines. Therefore, by virtue of their language, the 'converted Panas' are not entitled to any reservation benefit.

Currently there are a lot of Christian convert as SCs working in the government sector, illegally availing the reservation benefits. Fearing that they might lose their job, anytime, if proper enquiry is conducted, they want to surreptitiously include their community in the reserved category list of STs. With reorganization of constituencies, the lone Lok Sabha constituencies, all Assembly segments, President of Zilla Parishad, Block Chairman and seats of Zilla Parishad members of the district have been reserved for STs, which is well according to the guidelines laid down by the Delimitation Commission. Due to the above arrangement, there is a fear among the Panas (SC) of losing their political clout over the Kandhs (ST).

The demand by the converted Panas for reservation benefit by identifying themselves as Kui speaking tribes and the political manipulations by their leaders is one of the major causes of tension in the area.

Christians (Converted from Scheduled Castes) don't have reservation, which affects them and is a problem throughout India. This is not a problem just in Kandhamal but needs to be dealt with.

Land

Politically aware, led by highly-placed officers and motivated by the Church, the Panas, over the years, have grabbed large tracts of land belonging to Kandhs of the area. As per the land holding regulations of the State, no non-ST can buy or take possession of land from a tribal owner (as it is in Mizoram State). The Panas as well as converted Panas are not entitled to retain land that originally belongs to a tribal owner. Due to stringent implementation of land regulations in the State, illegal possessors of tribal lands in this district, mostly Panas and Convert Christians, are afraid of losing their land. Hence, they contrive somehow to get ST status, so as to be able to retain the land grabbed from the Tribals. Majority of the Churches in the district have been constructed on land either illegally grabbed from the Tribals or on the government Khasland. With increasing awareness among Tribals, the Christians now fear trouble and have been making frantic efforts to retain the land by changing the land records. "Suspicion among the scheduled tribe and scheduled caste inhabitants of Kandhamal is the main cause of riots with the Tribals suspecting that 'Pano' Dalits were capturing their land through fraudulent means,"[9] Justice Mohapatra said.

(Even today landlords exploit the Dalits. They are always under debt. Consequently we have many cases of farmers' suicides. North West India Christians have become landless labourers. Especially in Punjab we have a Jatt community who own most of the land. There are a number of incidents that tell us how they have been exploiting the Dalits.)

Cultural Onslaught

The Kandhamal district is a mountainous forest region having poor communication, education and health infrastructure. The Christians have been trying to divide the tribal community by teaching "My god is your god, but your god is no god". Presence of such divisive elements and such unreasonable and outlandish activities should not be allowed in such "scheduled areas" of the country as such violates indigenous

---

[9] *http://www.en.wikipedia.org Religious_violence_in_orissa* Dated. 06-01-2011.

culture, traditions and moorings of the people. The Tribals of the area are basically nature worshipers and hold Dharani Penu (Mother Earth) in high esteem. Their culture (Kulaachaar) is eco-friendly.

A brief case presentation of the North West India situation

This time North West India Malerkotla, Punjab went through a bout of communal violence though Malerkotla is a place known for communal harmony as it was Nawab of Malerkotla who had saved the children of the 10th Guru Govind Singh and hence Sikhs did not harm Muslims of Malerkotla even in 1947 partition riot and this is the only district in Punjab from where Muslims did not migrate to Pakistan.

On September 12th 2010 bout of communal violence took place after the Qur'an burning threat episode in the US. Since a Christian priest in the United States was to burn copies of Qur'an a church was vandalized in Malerkotla after the Eid celebrations. The police had to impose curfew. The angry mob also burnt a police motorcycle. The police had a tough time controlling the angry mob. Mufti Fazlur Rehman who appealed for peace said that the disturbances were politically motivated. He also maintained that events were pre-planned. After the news of disturbances in Malerkotla, the Christians in Ludhiana blocked the entire area and similarly Muslims also gathered near Jama Masjid in Ludhiana to protest against the burning of Qur'an in US. The unruly mob set ablaze the office of the forest department and two police vehicles in Poonch and after four people were injured when police fired warning shots in the air and lobbed teargas shells. In Jammu region the mob burnt effigies of Barrack Obama. Again the church had to go through a time of trouble when one of the schools of Amritsar Diocese, CNI was burnt down to ashes at Tangmarg Srinagar. This school was one of the best and beautiful schools of the region which was set to a blaze.[10]

Amritsar Diocese went through a tough time because of a riot in Batala and a CNI church was burnt down by the mob. The Epiphany Church at Batala, Gurdaspur district, Punjab was set on fire by some

---

[10] Personal Interview with Rt. Rev. P.K. Samantaroy, (Bishop Diocese of Amritsar, CNI), Dated: 12-01-2011.

Hindu extremists following a protest by local Christians against defamation of Jesus Christ by a picture showing Jesus with a cigarette and a beer can.

On 20th of February, 2010 the church building was totally ransacked and devastated; its ancillaries and interiors were totally damaged and burnt. The Bibles were burnt and reduced to ashes; the furniture in the vestry had been burnt and broken to pieces. The whole inner part of the building had been blackened because of the blazing fire. Some elements of fundamentalist forces of a majority community fumed its hatred on the Church building of a minority community to defuse its existence and identity. We call ourselves a secular state and portray ourselves as example of a secular democracy with multiple cultures and religions but the same communities of the same nations hate each other so much that we are unable to tolerate each other. We have to build our nation and that is possible only through peaceful co-existence and mutual cooperation.

It is unfortunate and shameful that so many riots take place every year in our country and hundreds lose their lives. Neither the State is serious about preventing these riots, nor building strong secular culture in our country. Our whole polity has been communalized and politicized. Are communal or secular parties responsible for all these riots? All our institutions have been affected by communal outlook. Police and administration has been deeply affected. Rashtriya Swayamsevak Sangh infiltration has taken place in all our institutions. Such communal clashes create a chaos and disorder in the society, eespecially in a country like India where people from different religions, castes, sects, and races exist

Historical Background of the Dalit Christians in Punjab

The rich heritage of the land of Punjab belonged to the aboriginal or indigenous people of this land, before the past two millenniums. These people were later subjugated and enslaved by the Aryans through various consecutive invasions. These people are now the Dalits. From then a form of slavery developed in this land in the social structure that it reduced the aboriginals to a level of subhuman condition. This also accounts for their present state of total dependency on others.

They were given very hateful and contemptuous nomenclatures like; *Dasa*, *'chandala'*, *'chamar'*, *'churah'*, *'bhangi'*, and *'Lal Bhegi'*,[11] etc. Down the historical line, this has transmitted its own social psyche which became inbred deep within these people and subsequently internalized their own slavery status in the society.

Similarities between the situation at Kandhamal and North West India

It won't be fair and right if we differentiate between the Dalits of India. Tribals and Dalits have been suffering for the last many centuries. So if we talk about the situation of Tribals and Dalits of India it's not very different. If we learn about the causes of the riots in Kandhamal and North West India we will surely come to know that their condition is quite similar. What happened in Kandhamal, isn't it all because of the power politics played and the conspiracy behind the conflict? Dalits and Tribals had to suffer in these riots and in the same way when the riots broke out in North West India, Dalit Christians had to suffer. Dalits and Tribals lost their lives and properties at Kandhamal in the same way as Dalits Christians of Northwest India were tortured and lost their school and Church. Time and again we hear the news that a Dalit has been beaten up badly for entering a worship place used by higher caste.

Problems of Dalit Christians prevailed even before the arrival of Christian missions in India. Dalits have been suffering due to the atrocities meted out to them by the so called higher caste. In a country where Dalits were persecuted irrespective of the religions they belonged to, it should therefore not surprise us when a higher caste from one religion persecutes people whom they rank as a lower caste from another religion. So the problem is basically age old, not emerged in recent times nor aggravated by any current shift in trend or attitude. Even today the Dalits in India it does not matter to which religion they belong to,, they suffer the same from the hands of the people claiming to belong to the upper caste.

---

[11] James Massey,*"Roots, A Concise History of Dalits"*, (New Delhi: CISRS-ISPCK, 1991), p. 9-10.

Moving Towards Peace

According to the 2001 census, Hinduism accounted for 80.5% of the population of India. Islam (13.4%), Christianity (2.3%) and Sikhism (1.9%) are the other major religions followed by the people of India. This diversity of religious belief systems existing in India today is a result of, besides existence and birth of native religions, assimilation and social integration of religions brought to the region by traders, travelers, immigrants, and even invaders and conquerors.

When we talk about peace, I strongly believe that the best example of peace and peacemaker we can ever have is the Lord Jesus Christ. Church doesn't have to go out to find peace because the peace is within the church itself. Church is supposed to be the instrument of peace. The Holy Bible says in the Gospel of Matt. 5: 9 "blessed are the peacemakers because they shall be called children of God." Here I would like to give a brief account of the Diocese of Amritsar as to how our church is moving towards peace. "The articulation of the common Vision of the Diocese of Amritsar, (CNI) was made at one of the Diocesan Conferences held at Shimla with view to give the Diocese a direction for its mission and ministry in future beyond the year 2000.[12]

The catch slogan emerged during the discussions was: that the diocese needs a diverse ministry of the whole people moving from 'pastor-centered' to 'people-centered', local and global, with all diversities integrated and all aspects included. The evangelical and spiritual renewal as central to the diocese, new ministerial formation, must aim at rejuvenating and mobilizing it's all ministerial wings and the congregations, progressing from 'self- indulgence' to 'sharing', and from 'dependence' to 'supporting.'

The Common Vision, as articulated, requires deep re-thinking for a common commitment to the discipleship of Jesus Christ who is the Lord and the Prince of peace. It needs developing of new models of integration based on enduring tolerance that would encourage participatory involvement of the people of other faiths too, and sharing of the diverse cultural heritage in the Indian context. Thus the people, in common, must focus on community building and promoting of

---

[12] *www amritsardiocese.org* Dated.03-01-2011.

general wellbeing of the whole creation through sensitizing and enabling people at the grass-root. Individual family can be the right starting point. There is a growing consciousness among the Christians that the Christian community must come out of its feeling of 'Minoritism' and gain more self-confidence and become pro-active in its approach to enter the mainstream of the nation in order to become effective agents of peace.

Church Response to Communal Violence

A statement like "If it is not hurting me why should I interfere in the situation at Kandhamal?" could be a common response that the church may have, if not openly, to riots or problems of the Kandhamal type in any part of the country. There is no unity among Christians; consequently we don't have a common voice on such issues. There should be some system or a common platform to bring Christians together. We should leave aside our doctrines and dogmas and come together in cases like these.

Some Christian organizations allure people to faith promising them a life free from problems, a community that does not discriminate on the bases of caste, an opportunity to send people abroad or admission in Christian institutions. Some Churches have pipe lines set abroad, the more they convert the heavier amount they receive as donation. Faith has been commercialized. The Church has to identify such people and severe relations with them.[13]

Church should be sensitive towards other faiths. Christian preachers should be sensitive to the people of other faiths and their religions especially during the time of open air preaching and conventions. We should be very careful and be mindful of the fact that we are living in a country of religious pluralism.

In our childhood we used to play a game where we used to make a line smaller without cutting or erasing it. We used to draw a parallel line larger than that, but in Christian faith we start cutting the line in order to make it short. This is the way we bring problems on ourselves.

---

[13] Telephonic Interview with Rev. Dn. Sandeep David, B.D. Graduate, Diocese of Delhi, CNI. Dated: 05-01-2011.

Mother Teresa never saw the religion of the people while serving the needy. Once when she was asked how she could minister to them, she replied "When I wash the wounds of the lepers and bandage them I feel I am ministering to Christ". This thought motivated Mother Teresa to serve people.

Church is called to serve the world irrespective of their caste, creed and colour. The bottom line is love. But in case of issues like Kandhamal we must reach, but in a positive way, towards such conspiracies. There has to be a forum, where all Christians throughout the country can be represented by their leaders and discuss about such issues. Christians have to have one voice in cases like these.

Tomorrow if any incident happens anywhere in the country can the Christians throughout the nation gather at Parliament Street in Delhi in peaceful protest to mount pressure on the Government to take prompt action? Just sending money or other help to the affected people is not enough but standing shoulder to shoulder in their miseries is all the more important.

Learning a lesson from the Riots

Learning a lesson from such incidents, Christian institutions must start educating Christian students even those who are not able to afford convent education. Today if we have Christian on high posts like IPS or IAS we will, to a great extent, manage to curb such violence against the community. But the pathos is that Christian institution grant admission to high caste students who come with thick wallets to educate their children who in turn, after their education start oppressing poor Christians. By this I don't mean to say that our institutions must discriminate on the ground of religion but there should be some policy to educate Christians, including the weaker section of society, so that tomorrow if such incidents happen we have people to control the situations.

When the Church is facing such situations, I strongly feel the urge and I would encourage the universal Church to pray like Reinhold Niebuhr (1892-1971) considering the situation of his time, who prayed as follows:

"God grant me the serenity
to accept the things I cannot change;
courage to change the things I can;
and wisdom to know the difference.
Living one day at a time;
enjoying one moment at a time;
accepting hardships as the pathway to peace;
taking, as He did, this sinful world
as it is, not as I would have it;
trusting that He will make all things right
if I surrender to His Will;
that I may be reasonably happy in this life
and supremely happy with Him
forever in the next.
Amen". (The Serenity Prayer)

Church's Response to Kandhamal and Similar Situations

- BISHOP YUHANON MOR MELETIUS

Friends,

We are now concerned of Church's response to Kandhamal and similar situations. My opinion on this has already been expressed in my Bible study earlier. The primary question with which I would like to begin in this context is, 'what does 'the Church' mean? To me, Church is 'an agency that tries to work out the liberation that Jesus inaugurated in this world'. This agency, therefore, has no fixed or permanent structure or shape. It is ever dynamic and vibrant and at the same time local. The best and most effective model for the Church to adopt to be an agency of Christ's liberation is 'the incarnation model'. John 3:16 portrays this model very well. It says, "God so loved the world that He gave (away) his Son ..." (the emphasis and bracket are provided and they talk about the methodology of the model).

The Church today has become an institution with its riches in many areas and the structures that keep and multiply these riches. Unless following the classic model the Church is ready to give away and shed these engulfing structures and come out into the midst of the people like Jesus did, it can not address the question raised here.

Jesus was called Son of God (by Peter), son of David (by the blind man on the road side), good teacher (by a ruler) etc. These were titles that would have put Jesus up on high pedestal. Indeed he was on the pedestal. However, taking up the mission of his Father, he came down into the midst of the people. During his time, anyone who was called a teacher stayed in the temple or in the synagogue. But as Jesus himself put it, such teachers 'put so much burden on the shoulders of the people and never cared to lift it even with their small finger'. Son of David to them was one on the throne with political power. Yes, he was Son of God, Son of God with us (the people); he was son of David as a 'good shepherd', he was a master who taught in the streets with words and deeds.

The Church has not learned much from the incarnation model. Rather, it copied the old model of the Jewish leadership, which was irrationally proud of its Mosaic authority and Abrahamic heritage. They forgot the fact that these two leaders were called by God to be 'with the people and be leaders in God's liberating act and be a blessing to generations'; not oppressors and enslavers. They were called for a mission with the people. They had no right to make their calling a proud claim of exclusivism and authoritarianism and to distance themselves from God's creation. The Church today has become highly institutionalized and structured. It is primarily concerned of maintaining status quo and keeping the structures and protects its interests. This is what the Church need to shed to come down in to the midst of the people.

The early fathers of the Church said, 'Jesus went through all the stages and situations of humans to liberate those stages and situations from bondage'. He participated in the life of humans with its most crude and concrete situations. He shared human's times of joy, sorrow, suffering, hopes and every other mood in this world. This is what the Church is called for. The incarnate Word asks his disciples to 'go out in to the world and be his witness'.

The response of the Church to situations like that of Kandhamal is 'incarnation'; to be present in body and spirit in every situation humans are placed in. This presence is fundamentally and essentially liberative in goal and purpose. Only that which is being incarnationally present can be liberative. The Church will 'walk with those humans who 'walk through the valley of the shadow of death' and will help them to resurrect. It is a participatory role. It will help people to face dangerous situations with determination and courage and to come out victorious and be resurrected. No one shall ever ask the Church 'Were you there when I was persecuted or when I was in jail or when I was hungry or when I was naked?' Church's presence and participation will help people take up the cross and to transform it to a sign of victory over every thing deadly. A Church that is tied up by institutional interests cannot engage in such a mission. Hence, the Church has to first come out from its castle, and then has to be present in the midst of the people. Situations like that of Kandhamal is a frequent possibility in today's world that is under the powerful influence of evil forces. Only the way of the cross can win over such situation and for that the Church, the steward of Jesus in this world, has to be present to bear that cross on behalf of the people.

Part III
BIBLE STUDIES

What Began in Kandamal Will End With Us!

Bible Study at the Consultation on 'Dalit-Tribal Interface: Healing and Restoration'

Organized by Council for World Mission with National Christian Council of India-COT and the Presbyterian Church in India.

Held from 17-22 January, 2011, at Bhubaneshwar, Orissa

CHILKURI VASANTHA RAO

Scripture Reading: Exodus 5:6-9

That same day the king commanded the Egyptian slave-drivers and the Israelite foremen: "Stop giving the people straw for making bricks. Make them go and find it for themselves. But still require them to make the same number of bricks as before, not one brick less. They haven't enough work to do, and that is why they keep asking me to let them go and offer sacrifices to their God! Make these men work harder and keep them busy, so that they won't have time to listen to a pack of lies." (TEV)

Setting

The Israelites in Egypt were a free people, but were gradually made to be slaves. Under Ramses II they were used to building granaries at Pithom and Ramses. The harsh rules as seen in the passage were made when Moses and Aaron requested on behalf of God to let the Israelites go (5:11).

I would like that we understand that the major part of Dalit Christians of Andhra Pradesh are in the plight as that of Israelites in Egypt.

On being a Dalit

Ask someone from Andhra Pradesh if he or she has heard the word *Banchan*. Ask for its explanation. Banchan is a word uttered by many of our Telangana rural people before they speak to someone of the so-called high caste.

The word is mispronounced by our illiterate populace. It is actually *Banisanu*, which means 'I am a slave'. The implied meaning is 'I am your slave'.

Since when have been our people uttering this word of total slavish surrender and submission to the so-called high castes? No one can remember nor can anyone trace, but it seems it has always existed from time immemorial.

In the utterance of the word *Banchan*, we observe we are not only made to be slaves we are made to accept slavery to be our profession and we are made to acknowledge that we are slaves ever.

Narration

Dolakala David, a SCMer from Ramakrishnapur, Andhra Pradesh explains what sort of lifestyle we were/are made to adopt as slaves:

- We were not supposed to wear upper garments

- We were not allowed to have footwear

- We were made to tie a palm leaf around our waist so that our foot prints might be wept off

- An earthen pot was hung around our neck to spit in

- Not allowed into the houses of the so-called high castes

- Always to speak with folded hands

- Always to address *Dora* (master), *Dorasani* (mistress)

- Nothing spoken without the prefix *Banchan*

The Kandamal experience

The Dalit Christians in the Kandamal region are not given freedom to worship, which is their basic right in the secular India. Their very social and religious identity is being questioned. They are pressurized by the local anti Christian elements to quit their houses.. Their legitimate rights are impinged upon.

Place of living

"The region of Goshen, where the Israelites lived, was the only place where there was no hail". (Exodus 9:26)

We see that the Israelites lived at a different place and not amongst the Egyptians. They lived in Goshen a place near the delta of river Nile. This place was in between Pithom and Ramses.

Where do we live as Dalits in our village settings? We have always been living outside the village. As the village grows and extends to the Dalit housing; the government allots new plots, and this has proved to be a plan to drive us further to the outskirts.

Being flocked at one place outside the village, it has always been easier for the so-called high caste people to attack us, burn our houses, rape our women and kill our men, as it happened in Tsundru, Karamchedu, Neerukonda, Padirikupam, Kanchikacharala and everywhere.

Narration

P. Sagar from Ramakrishnapur, Andhra Pradesh explains what happened to the Dalits Christians in Tsundur.

A heinous crime was committed by the so-called high caste Reddy community on Dalit Christians of the Lutheran Church in Tsundur, Andhra Pradesh.

The Dalit Christians were dependent on the Reddy community for their sustenance as agriculture laborers. But the Dalits' gradual upcoming in the fields of education and employment was not tolerated by the Reddy community. They were waiting for an opportunity to curb the independent behavior of the Dalits.

On the fateful day of 6th August 1990, the Reddy community in collaboration with Reddies of neighboring villagers has plotted against the Dalits. On the pretext that a Dalit youth misbehaved in the cinema hall and also disrespected the Reddies; the Reddies surrounded the secluded and isolated hamlets of the Dalits and brutally massacred eight youth with spears and daggers. One was even cut into pieces, stuffed into a gunny bag and thrown into a nearby water pond; while a heavy stone was tied to weigh it down, lest the gunny bag should float.

The Kandamal experience

The place of living – Though the Pana Christians and the Tribal Hindus are of the same social lot and live with each other in a much related manner, in and through the process of violence we recognize the forces that are driving them to the outskirts. We have seen the housing on the outside of the village, many are still living in the makeshift arrangements and even in the forest with much fear.

For peace to be restored efforts should be made that the housing be encouraged and helped to be where they belong in the village and are not to be made to live in isolated outskirts. Communal interaction and mutual growth must be encouraged with cultural blend and mutual economic growth.

Work

"Stop giving the people straw for making bricks, make them go and find it for themselves" (Exodus 5:7)

There was no *reserve* of straw for the Israelites for making bricks. It had become a rule and law that they had to find their own straw in order to bake bricks and make a living. Dalit Christians are also deprived of the government *reservations*. Education and Employment opportunities are closed and living is made hard. One has to look for one's own means of livelihood and no assistance is extended. The injustice is grave. While Dalits of Sikh, Buddhist and Hindu faith enjoy reservations privileges, the Dalit Christians are denied of the same.

The only employment that is offered in the village is to be a *pa-lay-ru*, annual bonded laborer, and for a meager payment of about Rs.

2000/- (rupees two thousand only) per year. This continues for years together because of the debt one incurs especially at the time of ill-health, marriages and deaths in the family. When the debt becomes high, even children join the parents in becoming *pa-lay-ru* to clear the debts and this vicious cycle had continued through centuries and continues.

Narration
Ms. Rajula from Tamil Nadu narrates what is means to be a *pa-lay-ru* and the inhuman treatment one meets.

Mohan was an annual laborer with a landlord. Mohan one day promised his master to get two bullocks from his cousin on rent to plough the fields the next day. The bullocks belonging to Mohan's cousin were taken to another village on work. Therefore, Mohan was unable to plough the field. The landlord having come to know of this, made Mohan and his pregnant wife play the role of bullock's and plough the field. Mohan's pregnant wife not being able to withstand the torture instantly died in the field itself!

The Kandamal experience
In the psyche of the so called upper castes, the Dalits and the Tribals are seen as their servants and cheap labor or even free labor. Their educational, employment and economic upper mobility is seen as a deprivation of that labor and thus through violence the Dalits are brought to square one in their lives. Thereby they are rendered dependent.

For peace to be restored we are need to take note that the medical, educational and social services that the church in this area was rendering were seen the wider community as servants serving the community. We were told by the hospital manger that persecution began after the closure of the hospital. Yes after the closure of the hospital the presence of the Christian community became redundant and there by persecution was justified. The church in the region must take note that credible social service schemes for the welfare of the society must be intensified in the region which asserts the importance of the presence of the church.

Government Machinery

Indian Scenario

The Constitution of India, Article 341 does not make any discrimination against the Scheduled Castes on the basis of religion. But the Presidential order called the "Constitution (Scheduled Castes) Order 1950" does it in the worst way possible. Para III of the order required all the Scheduled Castes to belong to Hinduism for availing the benefits that are guaranted to the Scheduled Castes in view of their socio-economic disabilities and educational and cultural backwardness which had no connection at all to their religious affiliations.

The Christian, Sikh, Buddhist etc. demanded the deletion of the communal clause vide para III of the Constitution (Scheduled Castes) Order 1950.

The Sikhs and Buddhists, who (like the Dalit Christians) faced social injustices, economic civil, political and religious discriminations became eligible for statutory and non-statutory benefits in the form of reservations in posts including the legislatures at the Senate and Central Government levels in 1956 and 1990 respectively while the Scheduled Castes Christians were left behind to fend themselves as objects of ridicule and despised with contempt.

"That the same day the king commanded the Egyptian slave-drivers and the Israelite foremen to stop giving straw" (Exodus 5:6).

"Then the king of Egypt spoke to Shiphrah and Puah, the two midwives who helped the Hebrew women, 'When you help the Hebrew women give birth' he said to them, 'kill the baby if it is a boy; but if it is a girl, let it live" (Exodus 1:15,16)

The king instructed the Egyptian slave-drivers and the midwives to treat the Hebrew harshly and even see to their death.

This is our experience too. Today when we go to a MRO, i.e. Mandal Revenue Officer or a MDO i.e. Mandal Development Officer for caste certificate and other needs, we are subjected to intense hardships. Incredibly we gaze at what is being done in depriving life to us.

It seems in the 1st generation we are Scheduled Castes originally, but in the 2nd generation treated to be Backward Class and in the 3rd generation placed into Forward class. What mobility, all to deprive life to us, deprive education, deprive employment and deprive all developmental opportunities.

Our MROs and MDOs have become agents of perpetuating unjust laws like the slave-drivers and the midwives of Egypt, appointed to ill-treat and drive us to death.

Narration

A Dalit Christian youth narrates his experience at the hands of MROs and MDOs especially when one goes for a caste certificate or other business.

I am M. Nelson from Ramakrishnapur, Andhra Pradesh. I was to write the EAMCET entrance exam. For this, I needed a BC-'C' certificate to avail the 1% reservation for Christians.

When I approached the MRO, I was rejected, stating that my grandparents were Christians and hence I was not eligible for BC-'C' certificate.

On insistence I was asked to wait for a week so that enquiries may be made to ascertain the facts. Two weeks passed, none came. When I approached the MRO I was asked to produce evidence that it was my father who got converted.

Having produced the evidence that my father got joined the Church; the MRO asked me to wait. I was getting impatient. I had to submit the application form. I went to the MRO after a week only to be asked to get evidence that my grandparents were not Christians.

When I had taken a letter to that effect the MRO insisted that an enquiry has to be made to see if my grandparents' names do not appear in our church records.

Being vexed I never approached the MRO again and I could not avail the 1% reservation.

The Kandamal experience

In the ruthless killings of the Kandamal Dalit Christians we see a nexus of the economic, religious and government officials nexus. The police are reluctant to file an FIR and if files it is wrongly filed. The doctors are abstain from giving a postmortem report. The Government officials are negligent of the massacres that are taking place in the broad day light.

For peace to be restored we have need to note that the legal way of justice must be ensured. Since "**no one is above law!**"; may it be the police, government officials, so called high caste persons, business magnets, religious fanatics, highly influential personalities, political figures, may it be any perpetrators of violence against Kandamal Dalit Christians directly or indirectly, all will be made responsible and thereby their participation will be curbed or least reduced to a minimum.

Concern for Fellow Dalits

"I have indeed heard the cry of my people, and I have seen how the Egyptians are oppressing them. Now I am sending you to the King of Egypt so that you can lead my people out of this country" (Exodus 3: 9, 10).

These are the words of God to Moses who was living in Midian away from his people who were suffering in Egypt.

Some or many of us by virtue of our parents migrating to cities either because of the harsh treatment in the villages or in search of employment or to study in the mission hostels etc. have come to live in cities away from our own people who are suffering under slavery and bonded labor. They are unable to get out of these shackles due to the stringent laws of the government which prevent them from any transformation.

But God calls us back to look at the plight of our people. Meet the Pharaoh/Government and lead them out into freedom and transformation.

Narration

Hear from a Rural Dalit Christian youth how he feels about who migrate to cities and live a well-off life and don't care about them who struggle living in slavery and suffering:

I am M. Sunil, born and brought up in Ramakrishnapuram. My father's brother was sent to study in a Christian school and boarding on a scholarship. He today works in a government hospital. His children studied in a convent school and are today working in private organizations.

The other day I went to participate in a rally for demanding SC reservations to Christians of Scheduled Caste origin. My uncle told me that we are Christians and no caste is attached to us. I told him that it is becoming extremely difficult to study and secure employment. He told me that suffering is part of our Christian faith.

The most unbearable painful thing was when he told me he was ashamed of us asking for reservations. It is quite shocking to learn of the attitude of our own people who were fortunate of coming up in life and do not realize that most of their own relatives have not got the opportunity as they had.

Dalit elites such as my uncle do not even care to help us unfortunate Dalits with a feeling of attributing nepotism and community chauvinism – God help!

The Kandamal experience
In the instance of Kandamal we are a wider family of faith with the Dalit Christians of this persecuted region. We must bear in mind that when one part of the body suffers all members suffer. The church then must shed its complacency and act, of course our action plan that is to be presented would suggest way and means of operation. If not, we must be aware that what began in Kandamal will end with us! AMEN.

I Am that I Am

Bible Study at the Consultation on
'Dalit – Tribal Interface: Healing and Restoration.'

Held on 17 -22 January, 2011

At the Crown Hotel, Bubaneshwhar, Orissa, India.
Organized by CWM in partnership with
NCCI and PCI

REV ZOSANGLIANA COLNEY

Text: Exodus 3:1-14

1.   BURNING BUSH/ I AM: The chapter of a burning bush, I think, is in someway relevant to the burning state of India!! Burning Orissa!! And this 'I AM chapter' be studied on the basis of eight 'I's found in these verses.

2.   GOD CALLS THE ENGAGED: Moses was keeping the flock of his father-in law (v.1) Moses heard the voice of the Lord at his workplace. God used to call those who were engaged in their own professions/ work place eg Nehemiah, Peter, Mathew and many others instead of calling those who were free or those who were sitting idle.

3.   GOD'S CALL: Do we know that we are approaching to God and God's call as we come over to Bubaneshwar in spite of various other attractions? Burning Orissa. . .To see the ruin of arson in Orissa which burnt Christians but not consumed!!

4. WE ARE COMING TO GOD: Do we know that we are approaching to God and God's call as we come over to Bubaneshwar in spite of various other attractions? Burning Orissa. . .To see the ruin of arson in Orissa which burnt Christians but not consumed!!

5. WE STAND ON THE HOLY GROUND: . . .the place on which you are standing is holy ground(v.5) Do we realize that our workplace is a holy ground? The holy place is the place where God's people are! Where the called one stands. God declared so.

6. WHO IS OUR GOD?: God wanted Moses to know the one who called him. One has to be clear about whom he serves. In the following verses God reveals Godself by using eight 'I's.

7. I AM, I SEE, I HEAR, I KNOW, I COME, I SEND, I WILL BE, I AM WHO I AM: Who is God, What God sees, what God hears, what God knows, what God does. . .

8. I Am: God revealed to Moses what kind of God is his God. I am the God of your father. . .

9. GOD SEES: I see: I have seen the affliction of my people.(v.7a) The God who sees the sufferings of the exploited. Our god is not like other gods. (they have eyes, but they see not. Ps 135:16b).

10. GOD HEARS: I hear: I have heard their cry because of their taskmaster (v.7b) The God who hears the cry of the helpless. Our God is not like other gods (They have ears but do not hear Ps 115:6).

11. GOD KNOWS: I know: I know their sufferings (v.7c) The God who understands the pain. (of sorrows, acquainted with grief Is.53:3)

12. WE ARE GOD'S WORKMATE: Do we share the ears/ the eyes of the Living God of Moses so that we can hear the loud cry of the suffering and affliction of the unprivileged, destitute, discriminate communities in our neighborhoods?

13. GOD ACTS: I come: I have come down to deliver them...(v.8) the God of actions. Our God is not the God who just hear the cry

and just see the suffering and only know the pain but the God who act upon what is heard and seen and known. (Moses must be happy that God move for action to rescue his people but...).

14.   GOD SENDS: I send: 'so come, I will send you to Pharoah'(v.10) 'without God we cannot, without us God will not'. God wants Moses and you to partner with God. It is a great privilege for us to be God's partners

15.   GOD WILL BE: I will be: When Moses put forward many excuses for being sent. God said, "But, I will be with you" (v.12). God is going to do and we are to represent God. Without us God will not!!

16.   I AM WHO I AM: I AM WHO I AM: (v.v.14)God will be Sovereign God now and forever. God will remain and withstand all kinds of attack, afflictions, atrocities, deprivations. Archbishop Benjamin Argak Kwashi of Nigeria while watching his house burning down by unbelievers was encouraged by Lord Jesus with his words, "Heaven and earth will pass away, but my word will not pass away" (Mat 24:34). I AM God is our portion as Psalmist says "The Lord is my chosen portion and my cup." (Pa 16:5)

Part IV

ORDERS OF WORSHIIP

"The God of 'I Am' Lead us To Peace and Reconciliation"

Order of Worship for 19-01-2011

Prepared by Dr. Hrangthan Chhungi and Led by Rev. Nancy

1.   **Call to worship:** *(As Miriam led the Song of Praises)*
     "Sing to the Lord, for he has triumphed gloriously".

     Yes indeed, God is the God of Love and in God's Love fears and hatred is subdued; peace, justice and reconciliation triumphed.

     The God of Justice is our strength, we shall not be moved.

     As children of God let us hear and remind ourselves as we commit to do the will of God through the words of King Lemuel's mother saying..."Open your mouth for the dump, for the rights of all who are left desolate. Open your mouth, judge righteously; maintain the rights of the poor and needy"

2.   **Prayer**
     O God of Love and Justice, we thank you for your bounteous mercy, love and care. As we are gathered together here we seek your continued guidance throughout our meeting. We commit our programme into your carelp us to discern what is right and just. Give us the courage to be the channels of blessings wherever peace and justice are robbed off from the people; and make us your instruments of peace and reconciliation even if the task seems to be mountain high. We pray this prayer in the name of the God whom we trust. Amen.

3.   Responsive Reading: *Psalms 77*

ied out to God for help;

I cried out to God to hear me.

All: **When I was in distress, I sought the Lord;**
at night I stretched out untiring hands,
and I would not be comforted.

Leader: I remembered you, God, and I groaned;
I meditated, and my spirit grew faint.

All: **You kept my eyes from closing;**
I was too troubled to speak.

Leader: I though about the former days,
the years of long ago;

All: **I remembered my songs in the night.**
My heart meditated and my spirit asked:

Leader: "Will the Lord reject forever?
Will he never show his favor again?

All: **Has his unfailing love vanished forever?]**
Has his promise failed for all time?

Leader: Has God forgotten to be merciful?
Has he in anger withheld his compassion?"

All: **Then I thought, "To this I will appeal:**
the years when the Most High stretched out his right
hand.

Leader: I will remember the deeds of the LORD;
yes, I will remember your miracles of long ago.

All: **I will consider all your works**
and meditate on all your mighty deeds."

Leader: Your ways, God, are holy.
What god is as great as our God?

All:	**You are the God who performs miracles;** **you display your power among the peoples.**
Leader:	With your mighty arm you redeemed your people, the descendants of Jacob and Joseph.
All:	**The waters saw you, God,** **the waters saw you and writhed;** **the very depths were convulsed.**
Leader:	The clouds poured down water, the heavens resounded with thunder; your arrows flashed back and forth.
All:	**Your thunder was heard in the whirlwind,** **your lightning lit up the world;** **the earth trembled and quaked.**
Leader:	Your path led through the sea, your way through the mighty waters, though your footprints were not seen.
All:	**You led your people like a flock** **by the hand of Moses and Aaron.**
4.	**Enactment:** *Prelude (as music being played...)*
Anita:	O My God! What on earth is happening to us! Look... look... at our neighbour's house, its burning, fire...fire..!! Daddy ... Mummy, where are you? O help me, help me, our house is also on fire...help ... some body help... Oh God... where is the door...no...No...am not able to open ...help...help...somebody help me......oh no...I can't see anything now, it's full of smoke now...where am I.... Oh God...I'm almost choked to death....Oh thank God...now I can breathe....
Sunjay:	oh no...no I can't run ... help me, somebody help me.... They are after my life!! Why are they chasing me? And

why are they after my life...?? What have I done...please please ....aaahh

(Sunjay was brutally injured and left alone as he could not run because he is limped due to polio attacked when he was a small kid...)

Bharathi: no...no... please don't do anything to my child...no...somebody help me...is there any one to help me.....

(Bharathi was able to snatch her child away from the hands of the violent mob...she was sobbing with fear....)

Narrator: *What we have seen and heard was the re-cap of the past violent incidents experienced by the Kandhamal community. As we know many have lost their lives, and many suffered inflictions of physical torture and mental trauma. The bush was burning indeed....but the bush was not consumed....!! The people of the Kandhamal Community are not consumed ...through frustrations, fears, trauma hounds them constantly...yet...there are some dim candles that continued to burn...having hope against hope...And now we are here as community of Church and Citizens who are committed to brighten those dimly burning candles and give hope to the fainted hearts ... to be instruments of peace and reconciliation for those who are victims of violence and victims of the perpetrators of violence who fall into the traps of the religious fundamentalists, who nurtured the divide and rule policies among the people of the Kandhamal community who once lived in a peaceful atmosphere as brothers and sisters... the challenge continues...let's journey together and raise our voices in this test of time....*

5.   **Song: (ALL) "Instruments of Peace"** *(the prayer of Frances of Assisi)*

(Chorus) *God make us instruments of your Peace*

> *Where there is hatred let your love increase*
> *God make us instruments of your Peace*
> *Walls of Pride and Prejudice shall cease*
> *When we are your instruments of Peace*

Where there is hatred we will show God's love
Where there is injury we will never judge
Where there is striving we will seek God's peace
To the people crying for relief
When we are your instruments of peace

Where there is blindness we will pray for sight
Where there is darkness we will shine God's love
Where there is sadness we will bear their grief
To the millions crying for release
We will be your instruments of peace

6. **Bible Study: Led by Rev. Zosangliana Colney, Executive Secretary, Mizoram Synod, Presbyterian Church of India**

7. **Prayer of Intercession**

1. Let us pray for the Community of Kandhamal Community (in Hindi)

2. Let us pray for the on-going Dalit-Tribal Interface (Malayalam)

3. Let us pray for the Council for World Mission (in Mizo)

4. Let us pray for the Presbyterian Church of India (in Oriya)

5. Let us pray for the National Council of Churches (in English)

8. **Litany of Thanks**

O give thanks to God, for God's steadfast love endures forever; God remembered us in our low estate, but God's love endures forever. God freed us from our enemies, for God's love endures forever. God gives food to every creature, for God's love endures forever. Give thanks to the God of heaven, for God's love endures forever

9. **Benediction**

"If you stand for a reason be prepared to stand like an Oak Tree; if you fall on the ground, fall like a seed that grows back to fight again"

And now May the God of Love give you the courage to Love those who are Loveless; May the God of Peace give you the courage to bring

Peace amidst violence; May the God of Reconciliation give you the courage to be the instruments of Reconciliation. May the God of Justice be your guiding light throughout your life; AMEN

Gospel and Culture Shaping Faith and Worship

Order of Worship – 21ˢᵗ January 2011

*Prepared by Raj Bharath Patta and led by
Ms. Gwyneth Morus Jones*

---

1.   **Call to Worship**

Leader: The Woman said to Jesus, "Sir, I perceive that you are a prophet. Our fathers worshipped on this mountain; and you say that in Jerusalem is the place where men ought to worship." Jesus said to her, "Woman, believe me, the hour is coming when neither on this mountain nor in Jerusalem will you worship the Father... God is spirit and those who worship him must worship in spirit and truth." (John 4: 21-24)

Come let us all join to worship God in spirit and in truth for God is Spirit and Truth.

People: **"The spirit blows where it wills, and you hear the sound of it, but you do not know from where it comes or to where it goes; so it is with every one who is born of the Spirit." (John 3: 8). Come into our midst O God the Spirit and be present amidst us in this world of ours, torn apart by violence, conflicts, fundamentalism, fanaticism, discrimination and oppression, and grant us healing building communities of solidarity and mutual interest across all our faith boundaries.**

2.   Opening Hymn: "*Worship the Lord...*"
(During which, the lamp shall be lighted. Offerings of Bible, turmeric, coconut and sprouted seeds shall be brought forward near the lamp.)

> *Worship the Lord, worship the Father, the Spirit, the Son*
>
> *Raising our hands in devotion to him who is one.*

1. *Raising our hands as a sign of rejoicing*
   And with our lips our togetherness voicing,
   Giving ourselves to a life of creativeness
   Worship and work must be one!

2. *Praying and training that we be a blessing*
   And by our workmanship daily expressing
   We are committed to serving humanity,
   Worship and work must be one!

3. *Called to be partners with God in creation*
   Honouring Christ as the Lord of the nation
   We must be ready for risk and for sacrifice
   Worship and work must be one!

4. *Now in response to the life you are giving*
   Help us O Father to offer our living
   Seeking a just and a healing society,
   Worship and work must be one!

3.   A Litany on Culture

1.   **Christians:** On becoming Christians, you Dalits & Tribals should leave all your pagan, gentile and indigenous cultures. Applying turmeric for your weddings and decorating your houses with turmeric, aren't they idolatrous and unchristian?

      Turmeric Powder: *I am yellow in colour, born and brought up as a root, nurtured with the mother earth, under tropical weathers and have been used by all humanity, irrespective of their region and ideology for several reasons. I am used as a lay anti-biotic curing several infections. I am used as a sign of auspiciousness. I am used as a mild ingredient in several recipes. I add grace to all the brides during their weddings.*

What harm did I do to the Christian brothers & sisters? Why is Christ against me and to the culture I am aligned with? Why am I branded as unchristian?

2. **Christians:** On becoming Christians, you Dalits & Tribals should leave all your pagan, gentile and indigenous cultures. Breaking of coconut during your festivals and auspicious occasions is a Hindu practise, and isn't it idolatrous and unchristian?

   Coconut: *I am green outside, brown in my penultimate cover, white in my inner layer with a pool of sweet nectar. I have been liked by all humanity irrespective of their region, religion and ideology for several reasons. I am used for my medicinal value, relieving skin problems. I am used as edible oil as well as healthy hair oil. I add beauty to the hair of the bride. What harm did I do to the Christian brothers & sisters? Why is Christ against me and to the culture I am aligned with? Why am I branded as unchristian?*

3. **Christians:** It was told by Christian missions in Orissa, that on becoming Christians they should leave their culture, which is pagan, gentile and indigenous. Dalits & Tribals converted to Christianity should not celebrate the festival called 'Rojo', which is celebrated before the sowing season begins. It was said Mother Earth is given rest for four days to regenerate herself, and the local folks symbolically sway in swings because they don't want even their feet to disturb Mother Earth. On the contrary, the converted Christians deliberately flout this custom and work on the fields, there by creating tension among the rest of the community.

   Mother Earth: *I am the green earth carrying the burden of all the creation in me. On tilling the soil, seeding the seeds, watering the fields, I yield fruits for the good of the creation. Indigenous festivals like Rojo, provides an opportunity to respect and acknowledge my hard labour in yielding the fruits. The indigenous people & I have been living like kith and kin serving for our mutual good. Festivals like Rojo make me happy, gives me the time to regenerate, celebrate, relax, and succour peace. As mother earth, what harm did I do to the Christian brothers & sisters? Why is Christ against me and to the culture I am aligned with? Why am I branded as unchristian?*

Together: God, in whom all beings, faiths & cultures exist and
           sustain, teach us to respect the indigenous cultures in our
           surroundings. Make our good news to penetrate into our
           cultures, similar to the incarnation of the Word becoming
           flesh. May we submit unto your will in responding
           positively to the rich cultural ethos of our lands. "And
           God saw that God's creation is good."(Gen 1:25b.) "What
           God has cleansed, you must not call common" (Acts 10:
           15). Grant us O God, the wisdom and sensitivity to see
           your goodness in your creation.

*(As a symbol of respecting our indigenous culture, we Christians shall share
turmeric powder with our neighbours, share the coconut pieces and also the
sprouted seeds from the mother earth)*

4.   *Bible Study:* Led by *Rev Dr C Vasantha Rao, Principal, ACTC*

5.   Affirmation of Faith: (*Together*)

By whatever name God is called, by whatever gender God is
identified, by whatever faiths God is worshipped, we all believe in
God, who is an embodiment of truth and love.

By whatever spectrum Jesus Christ is reflected, by whatever ideology
Jesus Christ is perceived, by whatever ethos Jesus Christ is
interpreted, we believe in Jesus Christ, who transcended the
boundary of faith in his mission, who dialogued with Samaritan,
who found faith in a Syro-phoenician woman, who built bridges
across cultures and faiths and who was always in solidarity with the
least, the lost and the last in the society.

By whatever cultures Spirit is understood, in whatever direction
Spirit moves, by whatever means Spirit works, by whatever tongues
Spirit speaks, in whichever context Spirit broods, we believe in Holy
Spirit, the giver of life, the one which gives meaning to life, the one
which builds friendship and solidarity among people of different
faiths and different cultures.

By whatever denomination a Church is called, whatever doctrine a
Church practices, in whichever locality a Church exists, by whatever
tradition a Church sustains, by whatever historical legacy a Church
marches forward, we believe in one Church built on the values of

the Reign of God, respecting other faiths, promoting justice, equality and peace within its purview, being a channel in building communities of peace and solidarity.

6.   Prayers of Solidarity

- *We thank you God for the ancient and great land of India, so full of natural beauty, of lofty mountains and mighty rivers, of forests and wildlife and myriad tongues, cultures, music, dance and art and architecture. We thank you for the rich heritage of literature and philosophy and religions.*

- *We thank you for the great stream of missionaries who brought the good news of Jesus Christ to India and shared it with people in cities and villages and remote corners. We thank you for their lives and their contributions that gave us hundreds of thousands of churches and schools and colleges, hospitals and orphanages.*

- *We thank you for our ancestors who listened to the good news, believed in it, accepted it and even suffered for it. These early Christians are a model for us who live as a large community of more than 25 million people spread all over this land. We thank you for large churches and for the many small churches and for those who still hear the Good News as sweet and full of hope and promise.*

- *Dear God, we come at this time with heavy heart. In the State of Orissa we hear the cry of innocent people being murdered and made homeless and living in fear. A small Christian community of very poor people are attacked and killed for no fault of theirs. Innocent sisters and brothers who provide education and healthcare and spiritual guidance are being attacked and killed.*

- *We seek the presence of your healing touch. You have taught us to love one another, even where hatred prevails. You have invited all people as brothers and sisters of your family. Speak to the people of India - people of all religions and cultures in this country to value love and peace, and not hatred and division that lead to senseless violence and long time enmity. Comfort all those who have lost members of their family, or hurt and living in fear. Give wisdom to leaders and the Government so that lasting peace can be achieved.*

- *God, this occasion calls us for an interface of gospel & culture, an interface of faiths & ideologies and an interface between Dalits & Tribals.*

Make us as messengers of your good news to be culture sensitive, respecting the indigenous cultures and building friendly bridges between gospel and culture. We also pray for your guidance for the Dalit & Tribal communities in India to be united in their efforts for liberation.

Together: **Lord God, we ask you to hear this prayer and grant us courage to face the challenges of our times and make us your proud disciples participating in the extension of your reign here on earth. In Jesus Christ's name we ask these petitions. Amen.**

7.   **Lord's Prayer:** *(Together) (Modified)*

Our God who is present everywhere, particularly in the struggles of our people,

Let your name be proclaimed by our acts of justice and truth,

Help us to realize your sovereignty by being in solidarity with one another,

Inspire us to do your will – to bring about transformation and be willing to die for others as you did.

Give us daily your knowledge to share our food, resources & ourselves with others, as you share them with us,

Lead us not into the temptation of practicing religious fundamentalism and being self-centered,

Deliver us from all kinds of oppression & discrimination

For your reign, power & glory shall come unto us when all of us live in the spirit of community governed by mutual dignity, respect and equality. Amen.

8.   **Benediction:** *(Together)*

May God, who created us all in God's equal image,

May Jesus Christ, who was in total solidarity with the struggling creation,

May Holy Spirit, who advocates justice to the creation

Continue to inspire, challenge and transform each of us here to go into the worlds to preach, profess and practice the values of God's reign and to strive for a just and inclusive community in our localities. Amen

9.   Closing Song: *"Jesus Christ is waiting..."*

1. *Jesus Christ is waiting*
   Waiting in the streets
   No one is his neighbour
   All alone he eats
   Listen Lord Jesus
   I am lonely too
   Make me friend of stranger
   Fit to wait on you.

2. *Jesus Christ is healing*
   Healing in the streets
   Curing those who suffer
   Touching those he greets
   Listen Lord Jesus
   I have pity too
   Let me care be active healing just like you.

3. *Jesus Christ is raging*
   Raging in the streets
   Where injustice spirals,
   And real hope retreats,
   Listen, Lord Jesus
   I am angry too
   In the Kingdom's causes
   Let me rage with you.

4. *Jesus Christ is dancing*
   Dancing in the streets
   Where each sign of hatred
   He with love, defeats
   Listen Lord Jesus
   I am dancing too
   In the Kingdom's causes
   Let me dance with you

Part V

APPENDICES

Appendix 1

Report of the Sub Committee to the Trustee Body

Frame of Reference:

Issues

1.   HIV/AIDS
2.   Oppressed Communities (Dalit and Tribal Struggles)

Area

1.   Africa
2.   South Asia

HIV/AIDS

Today being the World AIDS day, it is indeed very appropriate that we as the Trustee Body of CWM reassure our solidarity with and our responsibility towards those infected with and affected with HIV/AIDS – individuals, families, communities and nations. Even as we are planning as to how we need to express our concerns, HIV/AIDS is ravaging Sub Saharan Africa taking away millions of lives. An estimated 29.4 million people are living with HIV/AIDS facing stigma, dehumanisation and the threat of death. In 2002 alone 3.5 million people have been newly affected with the disease in Sub Saharan Africa. While the past year has claimed 2.4 million Africans, 10 million youth and three million children are living with HIV/AIDS in this region. It is very essential that we continue to act and address this issue in more effective ways now as these societies will be facing the worst impact of HIV/AIDS during the next ten years and beyond. It would also be good if CWM can pledge today that we together as individual member churches and as CWM will look at different ways in which we can network with local, national and international bodies and work on this world's most deadly disease. In line with this year's theme of World AIDS day – **Stigma and Discrimination,** it is necessary to affirm and act with conviction that it is equally important to combat the stigma and discrimination related to HIV/AIDS as it is to develop medical cures that focus on preventing and controlling. The next year's theme of World AIDS day is **Women and AIDS** and our response to this will speak louder on our faith and action.

HIV/AIDS has swept away the progress made by the Sub Saharan region in the last few decades since it has been discovered in 1981. This has brought down the average life expectancy of the people of this region from 62 (without AIDS) to 47! It dramatically affects labour, forcing a setback on education, social progress, economic activity and cultural ties. In this context, the Church becomes a place where many look for social, spiritual and moral support.

The rationale to choose this continent for our frame of reference is that this continent is the most affected and CWM has had its work here for the last few years on HIV/AIDS. The positive benefits of this programme can be shared with the other regions of CWM as according to the intensity of the problem.

Oppressed Communities (Dalit and Tribal Struggles)
The Dalits constitute about 25% of the Indian Population numbering about 240 million. The government census itself puts it between 16 – 19 % with much reluctance after forcefully gathering a sizeable percentage under the Hindu religion. Similarly, the percentage of Tribals is also put reluctantly as eight (80 million) when the actual percentage is much higher than this. India has one of the largest Tribal populations in the world.

South Asia is a region which has become traditionally caste based. The communities are segregated into two segments of people – the small minority who constitute the upper caste and the vast majority forming the oppressed communities – the Dalits and the Tribals. Caste system has been practised in this region for the last 3000 years. While the Tribals are the victims alienated from their rightful habitat, their livelihood and their self identity, the Dalits being victims of the above mentioned also face the dehumanisation on account of social ostracisation through untouchability. Untouchability expressed in the form segregation, dehumanisation and denial of human rights operates on the basis of the concept of purity and pollution, propagating stigma and discrimination. Through the Missionary intervention of the Church, these oppressed communities have been brought into the forefront of social upliftment by the preaching, healing and teaching ministries. This social empowerment of the Dalits and the Tribals particularly through education has created an enormous suspicion in the minds of the dominant castes and the religious fundamentalist groups who for their convenience would like to keep the Dalits and Tribals in the darkness of their ignorance. Under these circumstances the church in the Indian Subcontinent faces extraordinary pressure from religious fundamentalists and caste fanatics (Hindus in the case of India and Muslims in the case of Bangladesh). A vast majority of the Dalits and Tribals are forcefully gathered under the umbrella of Hindu religion to make this religion appear as the religion of the masses of people in this region. The Dalits and the Tribals are denied the freedom to choose their religion and faith. Therefore it becomes important for CWM to express its concern and solidarity with this region to enable the member churches to work together to address this issue towards achieving dignity and Total Human Liberation.

As 75% of the Indian Christians are Dalit Christians, the Indian Church itself is genuinely a Dalit Church. While it is a sad situation that discrimination on the basis of caste is practised even within the church, the Church in the recent times is also threatened against embracing these oppressed communities and challenged to accept Varna Dharma i.e. discrimination on the basis of caste by imposing the various laws against conversion and promoting Saffronisation within the educational system. The Indian Church being a Dalit Church has a greater responsibility to address the Dalit issue on behalf of the whole Dalit people. Therefore, it becomes very important that the CWM stands in solidarity with the Church in the South Asia region to struggle against the caste demon.

Statement on HIV/AIDS
The CWM Trustee Body, meeting in London on November 24 –

December 1, 2003, takes note of the profound and worldwide suffering amongst those people living with, dying from and affected by the HIV/AIDS pandemic. The Trustee Body expresses its prayerful solidarity with all the CWM member churches and with the Africa region churches in particular, as together we seek more effective ways to combat, contain and ultimately overcome the disease and its devastating effects. As CWM we affirm our belief and trust in a loving God and refute all notions about HIV/Aids being the result of God's judgement and punishment.

The Trustee Body wishes to commend and to encourage the CWM member churches in their manifold efforts and initiatives in response to the HIV/AIDS challenge within their respective countries and contexts. The Trustee Body however believes that CWM globally, regionally and nationally is called at this time to embark on the following strategies to strengthen, resolve, increase capacity and improve effectiveness in the quest to combat HIV/AIDS.

- Maximise and strengthen existing networks
- Form new alliances and partnerships
- Share information, knowledge and insights more widely
- Commit additional resources

It is recommended that the Trustee Body appoints a CWM HIV/AIDS working group (WG), which shall be based in Africa, to undertake the following task and to report back to the Trustee Body in June 2004.

Awareness building

An update on the methods of advocating the facts about HIV/AIDS to eradicate the fear in the minds of the people about the HIV/AIDS and the affected people

A plan of action to erase the stigma and discrimination

Combating HIV/AIDS

A research and report on the possible ways of networking with other Churches, Christian and secular organisations at local, national, regional and global levels for an increased level of participation in the prevention, care treatment and treatment of HIV/AIDS

To provide more information on the support systems available to combat the epidemic of HIV/AIDS

Prevention and Treatment

Identify the prevention methods/efforts used within this region and determine the extent to which the member churches are working together with other agencies and how these networks could be enhanced.

> A survey of the additional support required to implement successful prevention and treatment
>
> Ways of promoting specific attention to women and young girls in relation to getting adequate information on HIV/AIDS and the prevention methods
>
> CWM'S role in ensuring a more healing and healthier world for the future generations.

Statement on Oppressed Communities (Dalit and Tribal Struggles)

The Trustee Body took note of the immense suffering in South Asia whereby people of the oppressed communities are discriminated against and marginalised on the basis of groupings, classes and castes. The Trustee Body expresses its prayerful solidarity with all the member churches in the South Asia region as they attempt to respond to the challenges of this situation.

As CWM we affirm that all people are equal in God's sight and that no human being, grouping or community should be regarded and treated as inferior to others or of lesser value. We encourage churches in South Asia to ensure that their own governing structures, organisational arrangements and mission activities do not exclude, discriminate against and marginalise certain people.

The Trustee Body believes that CWM globally, regionally and nationally is called at this time to respond to this challenge in a more substantial and sustained way. To this end, it is recommended that the Trustee Body appoints a working group which shall be based in South Asia, to undertake the following tasks, and to report back to the trustee body meeting in June 2004.

Awareness Building

Report on the Caste related issues – the impact of the dominant religion, its fanatic ideas and practice of untouchability.

> Report on the magnitude of the problem of untouchability within South Asia especially within the churches and the Churches' effective ways of dealing with these issues.

Report on the impact of the dominant religion on the Tribals in relation to the socio-economic and religio-cultural issues.

> Report on the role of Dalit and Tribal women's issues that make them the most vulnerable.

Combating Oppression

Research on steps to enhance networking with Dalit and Tribal liberation groups both within the Christian circle and the wider circle of Dalit and Tribal Communities

> Outline methods to promote a dialogue with the dominant groups to achieve religious freedom and human liberation.
>
> Ways to network with the other backward communities to strengthen up the liberation movements against caste and untouchability practices.
>
> Plan of action for CWM to express its solidarity in ensuring that the Dalit rights are recognised as human rights and the value of their culture and religion is recognised and restored.
>
> Plan of action for CWM to ensure the right of Tribals to the religion and faith of their choice and the value of their culture and religion be recognised and restored.
>
> Outline 'Plan of action' for CWM to ensure that the Tribals are not displaced from their habitats on account of development policies which work at the cost of their lives and livelihood. Ways of conserving nature, and recognising the role that they play in this venture be worked upon.

Rev. Lala Rasendrahasina
Dr. Pauline Sathiamurthy
Rev. Dr. Desmond van der Water
Mrs. Elizabeth Joy   1.12.03

Decision taken by the TB

Therefore, taking into consideration the magnitude and the urgency of these issues and the grave situations which are an affront to human dignity, respect and the right to life, it is recommended that the two working groups be assigned with the above responsibilities. The working groups shall be constituted with one member from each of the constituent churches, and shall determine their own modus operandi but in consultation with the CWM General Secretary. The Trustee Body agrees in principle that in the event of financial resources needed for the working groups activities to achieve the above tasks, the CWM Moderator, Treasurer and General Secretary shall be consulted.

Appendix 2

Kandhamal:
Restore Justice,
Peace and Reconciliation

'That they may be One' John 17: 21

Statement of the International Conference,
Bhubaneshwar 17—22 January 2011

We the church and civil society in India, express our anguish at the continuing injustice and violence inflicted on the vulnerable sections of our society, especially the tribals and the Dalits. We condemn the everyday atrocities on them, some reported and many more unreported, in the guise of 'development', 'security', 'custom', 'tradition' and 'culture', and exacerbated by the impunity afforded to the perpetrators. We note with concern the increasing militarisation of state response to the legitimate democratic aspirations of these historically discriminated peoples when they attempt to exercise their constitutional rights.

We recognise the nexus of international capital including the market, religious, communal and caste forces as active instruments in the oppression of Dalits, indigenous and tribal peoples the world over, and their role in creating conflict, pitting the victims against each other. The resilience and resistance of these vulnerable communities poses a challenge to each of us, individually, collectively and institutionally. We stand in solidarity with them amidst their pain and struggle.

Kandhamal is a specific instance of this injustice and we acknowledge the unpreparedness and fear of the church in dealing with the situation. The church needs to urgently develop transparent, accountable governance systems for early warning and response and the capacity for performance based management so that available solidarity can be best utilised.

We denounce the complicity of the government and hold both the state and central governments accountable for their delay in action and inaction. We were prevented from providing even humanitarian relief to the victims by illegal executive fiat. Our visit to Kandhamal and the interaction with the communities overwhelmed us with the pain and the plight that the survivors still have to endure with continued threat to their life. The murder of Pradhan, a Lay preacher in Banjamah village as recently as 10 January 2011 has once again stirred up a lot of heat and dust in the Christian communities and once again has heightened the insecurity.

We are shocked at the present and continuing victimisation of the survivors of the Kandhamal persecution, three years after the attacks, the scale of deprivation and the depth of institutionalised hostility to their rehabilitation. We realise that peace is not possible without justice, and justice is not possible where impunity reigns and crime rewarded. The culpability of the state, up to the highest levels, in subverting the rule of law cannot be ignored. It is the primary responsibility of the state to protect, promote and secure human rights and dignity. We urge the state to initiate confidence building processes immediately by rebuilding all homes and places of worship and providing security to the people to freely live and practice their religion with secure livelihoods.

We appeal to the broader society to take cognisance of divisive forces and not fall prey to narrow sectarian propaganda, but to rise collectively to protect the human rights and dignity of all. The role of the media and enlightened sections of society in this regard is crucial in preventing the general slip of society into fascism and apathy.

We will continue to challenge the fascist ideologies, fundamentalist forces educating and empowering all citizens to be free and equal, rejecting ideologies of social stratification and inequality even when they are clothed in the language of cultural nationalism and liberal ideologies, informing citizens of their rights as enshrined in the constitution and support them as they attempt to exercise their rights. We pledge to help rebuild not just their homes but their lives and their communities in solidarity and atonement in an inclusive process of healing. We rededicate ourselves, with redoubled effort and commitment, for social justice and empowerment of these communities.

" Dalit & Tribals together becomes the healers of the society as they seek healing" could have been scripted in the statement, besides the new action plans that were

Action points

1. Build community to community, lateral links and communication channels for solidarity among the oppressed working through civil society networks.

2. Be a watchdog, be proactive in identifying tension spots and work to defuse.

3. Work for human rights of all not only Christians.

4. Work on new media

5. Have small media watch groups in different cities (response to both print and online editions)

6. Social audit of the church response (including identification of victims, survivors, beneficiaries and the support received).

7. Transparent handling of church funds

8. Have a self-reflection on the role of the church and the crisis of credibility.

9. Is 'turning the other cheek' due to fear of exposure or conviction?

10. Engagement with the state, and entering into institutions of governance.

11. Church needs to be empowered to be a missional church with social engagement with various socially relevant projects to the poor of the local larger society.

12. Recommend the theological colleges for having human right as part of their curriculum.

13. NCCI to take up the murder case of Pradhan and work of providing security and restore justice.

14. Follow up plan for the future: - To find a credible anchor in the local set up such as Ms Roshanara, Mr. Akshay and others.

    - To find credible ambassadors like Mr. Ramdayal Munda and Mr.HarshMander, Mr.KP.Sasi (Direndra Panda-09437385757, email-dhirandrapanda@gmail.com)

    - To help promote community to community links and instil a sense of security.

    - To request Mr. Gladston Xavier to share the documentation of the cases and the process.

15. Peace process may be continued with time to time evaluation of how Progress of relationships made between Dalit Christians and Dalits of other religions, the Tribal Christians and Tribals belonging to other religions: Intra-Dalit and intra Tribal and between the Dalit and the Tribal communities.

16. Peace – Curriculum be prepared for the schools in Orya and Hindi languages as a pilot project for the Orissa State.

Ms. Elizabeth Joy   **Dr. Hrangthan Chhungi**
Executive Secretary   *Executive Secretary*
Mission Education   *Commission on Tribal & Adivasi*
Council for World Mission   *National Council of Churches in India*

Rev. Lalramliana Pachuau
Senior Administrative
Presbyterian Church of India
January 21, 2011

Appendix 3

Photo Gallery

*Rt Rev Samson Das, Bishop of Cuttack Diocese, CNI,
welcoming the Participants*

*Mrs Elizabeth Joy, the Executive Secretary for Mission Education, CWM leading
the lighting of lamp during inaugural Worship. Others from left to right –
Rev Dr Roger Gaikwad, Mrs Enna Nsofu, Bishp Subas Chandra Gouda, Bishop
Samson Das, Rev S S Majaw, Bishop Yuhanon Mor Meletius*

Bible Study led by Bishop Yuhanon Mor Meletius, Metropolitan of Trissur Diocese, Malankara Orthodox Syrian Church

Dr Kaushal Panwar, Assistant Professor of Sanskrit, Delhi University. delivering the Keynote Address

The Participants with rapt attention to the keynote address

Panel Discussion on "Legal battle: Pinning down the perpetrators to move forward promoting peace, justice and reconciliation". Panellists are Adv B.D.Das and Adv Sheila. Session moderated by Adv Anjna Masih

Panel Discussion on "Causes of the Kandhamal violence 2007/2008".
Panellists are Mr Aksheya Kumar, Dr John Dayal and Fr Ajoy Singh.
Session moderated by Mr Angelious Michael

Morning Devotion led by Mrs. Enna Nsofu, CWM followed by a Panel
discussion on Church's Response for "Healing and Restoration Towards,
Peace, Justice and Reconciliation for Dalit and Tribal Communities". Panellists
are: Bishop Samson Das, Rev Dr Roger Gaikwad &
Rev Laldawngliana. Moderated by Dr (Mrs) S Manohar Rao.

Feedback session led by Rev.Dr.Ch.Vasantha Rao & Rev. Raj Bharath Patta

Morning Worship led by Mrs. Gwyneth Morus Jones, CWM

A Bible Study led by Rev. Zosangliana Colney,
Executive Secretary, Mizoram Synod, PCI

Panel Discussion on "Healing and Restoration Towards Peace, Justice and
Reconciliation of the Dalit and Tribal Communities in India – Role of Christian
Organizations and Theological Education". Panellists: Rev Vincent Rajkumar &
Bishop A S Hemrom. Session Moderated by Mr Kasta Dip

Panel Discussion on "Roles of Christian Media as Channel of Healing and Restoration towards Peace, Justice and Reconciliation for Dalit and Tribal Communities in India" Panellists: Prof. Mammen Varkey (Chief Editor People's Reporter), Mr Anto Akara (ENI Correspondent) and Mr Dibin Samuel (Senior News Person, Christian Today). Session moderated by Mr Edwin Daniel

Group Presentation on "Dalit and Tribal Women - Instruments of Peace and Reconciliation amidst Violence" Presenters: Mr Angelious Michael, Ms Rosnara and Ms Masophi Kengoo. Session Moderated by Adv Brother Markose

Church's Response on "Healing and Restoration Towards, Peace, Justice and Reconciliation for Dalit and Tribal Communities". Panellists from left to right: Rev Nathaniel B M., Bishop Yuhanon Mor Meletius, Bishop Bijaya Naik Kumar and Rev Nancy Singaram. Session moderated by Ms Ibatista Shylla

An Exposure Trip and solidarity visit to Kandhamal on 20 [th] January 2011. Mr Kasta Dip gives an orientation to the georgaphycal locations of Kandhamal, places of destruction and the victims of violence.

A time of interaction. Listening the testimonies of the victims of perpetual violence against Christians of both the Dalits & Tribal Communities in Kandhamal area.

The Moorshed Memorial Christian Hospital in Kandhamal, where hundreds of the victims of 2008 violence took shelter inside the Hospital for safety, for medical care and counselling. Though the hospital barely has the required and needed facilities in terms of infrastructure and personal staff, yet it serves as a Holistic Centre for the needy in this Tribal belt of Orissa State. To respond to this urgent need of the medical staff after the violence broke out, the Mizoram Synod, Presbyterian Church of India has sent three Doctors, One Nurse and one Evangelist at MMC Hospital, who are now serving in this hospital.

Stealing some moments of laughter amidst the reality of pain

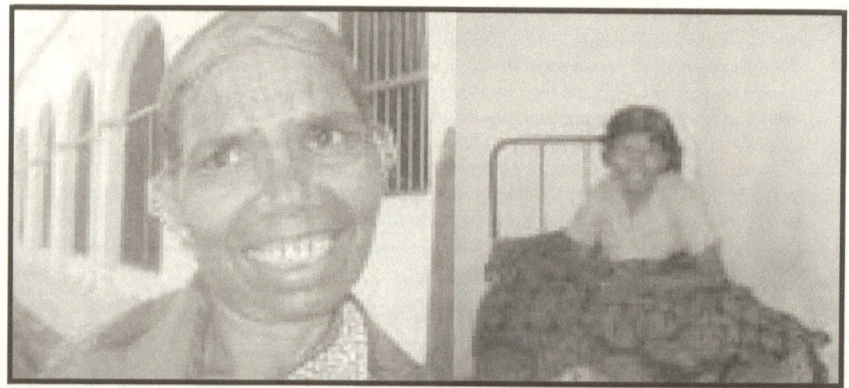

After 3 years of destruction and violence, its hard to get back to normalcy as the stint of the violence remains with unrepaired houses and church buildings still lying in many places even as a few houses and church b uildings are under repair.

Bible Study: Rev. Dr. Ch. Vasantha Rao, Principal, ACTC, Hyderabad and chaired by Rev. Nancy Singaram

Speech on "Kandhamal Riot: Response from the Government for Healing and Restoration" by Dr H T Sangliana, Vice-Chairperson, National Commission on Minorities, Govt. of India, New Delhi and chaired by Rt Rev Dr B.S.Devamani

*Final plenary, a time of feedback and discussion on action plan guided by
Rt Rev Dr Devamani, Mrs Elizabeth Joy and Rev Dr C Vasantha Rao*

*Felicitation of Mrs Elizabeth Joy who is completing her 8 years of service at
CWM as the Executive Secretary for Mission Education by Rev Laldawngliana,
former Secretary of SARC, CWM and mementos presented by Dr.John Dayal*

*Felicitation and presenting mementoes to Mrs. Enna Nsofu & Mrs. Gwyneth
Morus John, members of CWM Trustee Body by Rev. Laldawngliana*

*Vote of thanks by Dr Hrangthan Chhungi, Executive Secretary,
Commission on Tribals & Adivasis, National Council of Churches in India,
Coordinator of the programme*

Where is this Christ, our drum, present?

Europe: This Christ our drum is present
                 In all realities of life
                 Disturbing those in comfort
                 Comforting those who are disturbed
                 Stretched far too much in life
                 As Dalits, tribes, indigenous, women
                 Christ questions all acts of injustice
                 Through his death on the cross
                 Inspiring the oppressed
                 Challenging all systems that profane
                 God's name, God's work and God's reign

Though we are from different cultures
Though we are from different races
Though we are from different places
Though we are of different languages
Though we are of different skin colours
Though we are of different sexes
We are one in Christ
So, let us celebrate
Celebrate our diversity in God

Let us come together to sound
Each in our own unique way
Each in harmony with the other
Just as the sound from these drums
Are different but also precious
And together in harmony abound.

We can retain our uniqueness
Still reflect God's image and likeness
In all our work, worship and play
That in God's love we may abound
Let us continue in God's mission
With renewed and revived mission.

Scripture Readings Old Testament
                    New Testament

How do you see the drum as a symbol in God's mission?

East Asia: It was here that CWM was born
                      Now thirty long years have gone
                      Drums are a uniting symbol
                      Drums are a liberating symbol
                      Drums have been there
                      From time immemorial
                      Drums are there in joy and sorrow
                      Drums are there today and tomorrow

                      Mission unfolds each and every aspect
                      Of proclamation, liberation and transformation
                      Drums are used to convey these with respect
                      Drums are part of every mission
                      To proclaim the death of slavery
                      To proclaim the joy of victory
                      Over all evil forces, and structures unjust
                      Based on caste, class, religion
                      Race, sex, colour or region.

To what would you compare the drum?

South Asia: What else but salvation, who else but Jesus Christ
                      Yes, a drum is very similar to Christ Jesus
                      Who, from every evil, saves each one of us.
                      A drum is made up of an animal skin
                      Stretched taunt on a hollow log.
                      Drum mediates between the human and the divine
                      Drum mediates between the humans
                      Drum mediates between the dead and the divine too.
                      Christ was stretched on the cross – the hollow log
                      As an animal, he was killed
                      In agony and pain, he did cry
                      As soldiers whipped and pierced him.
                      Jesus' voice from the cross still resonates
                      As the most beautiful sound - from any drum
                      Thus Christ mediates between the human and the divine
                      Christ mediates between the humans
                      Christ mediates between the dead and the divine too.

Contributors

Ms. Ibatista Shaila is a native of Nongpoh, a small town between Shillong and Gauhati. She is the third child of Rev. M.S. Shadap and Mrs. R.J. Shylla. She did her Bachelor of Divinity (BD) from United Theological College, Bangalore. Currently she is the Programme Secretary of the YWCA, Bangalore. She has served the Student Christian Movement of India  as the Study Secretary of Women's Desk. Her strength lies on her passion to work for the upliftment of women and children and care for the neglected. She is a down to earth person who works with a smile and a song, very approachable, cordial and one who works with great commitment to make her dreams of a non-hierarchical society come true.

Mrs Ennah Nsofu is a member of the United Church of Zambia. She has taught in the Ministry of Education for two years and was also involved in community development for about twenty eight years. Currently she serves as the member of the Board of Governance of the Theological College of UCZ. Additionally, she is also the Committee  Member of the Women Christian Fellowship and representative of CWM's Africa region. She is also a member of the CWM Trustee Body since 2006.

A young and dynamic leader, **Mr. Angelious Michael** has several feathers in his cap. He is the Vice President, NCCI; presently the Program Secretary - Youth Desk, JELC and Coordinator - Partnership Desk, JELC. In addition to all these, he is a member of the World Council of Churches' Commission on Education and Ecumenical Formation and is also Participant of the Ecumenical Water Network. Michael is an active Contributor to the youth work of the Lutheran World Federation.

Advocate Anjna Masih has a B.Sc and L.LB from Delhi University and is enrolled with the Bar Council of Delhi as an Advocate. As an advocate by profession, she has been using her expertise serving Christian Organizations in Delhi. Her specialization is Matrimonial Laws. She was the Executive Secretary, Commission on Policy, Governance & Public Witness of the National Council of Churches in India based at Delhi Office during the last two years. She is also actively involved in various Capacity Building Programmes and Seminars as Resource Person.

Mr. Anto Akkara has MA in English literature and LL.B degree from Delhi University. Anto has been a journalist for two decades with international media and has traveled extensively to troubled spots in South Asia. For last 12 years, Anto has been South Asia correspondent of ENI (Ecumenical News International from Geneva) and a correspondent for CWM. He has to his credit over half a dozen national and international media awards for his outstanding reporting on social and human rights concerns. His two recent books, titled **'Kandhamal - a blot on Indian Secularism'** and

'**Shining Faith in Kandhamal**' stirred the conscience of the nation with his critical analyses and creative writing. His passion and commitment for the cause of the downtrodden is so deep and is reflected in his interactions, relationships and writings. He witness through his writings shapes the faith of many!

Rev. Raj Bharath Patta is a young and dynamic ordained minister from the Andhra Evangelical Lutheran Church (AELC) and is currently serving as the General Secretary of the Student Christian Movement in India. He held an important role at the National Council of Churches in India (NCCI) as the Executive Secretary for the Commission on  Dalits for the last five years. He is a prolific writer with poetic touch. He is known for his Bible Studies and creative Liturgy for the Order of Worship. His book on "A Violent Sight on a Silent Night" is an impressive theological reflection on the reality of the Kandhamal massacre of 2007/2008.

The Rt Revd Dr BS Devamani, (BA., BD., STM (New York), D. Min (Chicago), D.D.(New York) is the Bishop in Dornakal with many responsibilities as a dynamic Church leader. Presently he is the Chairman of Laity Work, Church of South India Synod and Chairperson – Dalit Commission, National Council of Churches in India. Previously  he served as - Director of PAD, Church of South India Synod, Ecumenical Relations. He also has conducted Holy Land tours for Clergy of all the Dioceses in Church of South India. He has a rich Pastoral Experience as Curate, Associate Priest of Canterbury Diocese in United Kingdom and a Full-time Presbyter in Emington, United Church – Illinois Conference, USA. He was also the Priest In-charge and Chaplain for Diplomats, Diocese of Jerusalem, Israel.

Bishop Yuhanon Mor Meletius is the Metropolitan of Thrissur Diocese of Malankara Orthodox Syrian Church. He is a very dynamic person and a Bishop with a 'Difference'. He believes in dialogue, change and liberation with respect to both himself as well as others from bondage (mental, physical and spiritual) within the varied structures that distort God ordained identities with freedom to lead a meaningful life. He was born in a small village in central Kerala district of Ernakulam in 1954. He is a graduate in Malayalam language and literature. He did his B.D. and M.Th (in Old Testament) at the United Theological College, Bangalore. He was Ordained as a priest in May 1986 and consecrated as Bishop in December 1990. He served as Vicar in a small congregation in the home diocese for 3 years. He taught at Malankara Syrian Orthodox Theological Seminary, Udayagiri, Ernakulam (MSOTS) for 9 years. Currently, he is a guest lecturer at St. Thomas Orthodox Theological Seminary (STOTS), Nagpur, Maharastra. He is a social democrat and activist. He is one who is always proud to identify himself as a Student in Old Testament despite the credit he has to both his Scholarship as well as teaching experiences!

Rt. Rev. Subas Chandra Goudo is the Bishop of Jeypore Evangelical Lutheran Church and the President of Utkal Christian Council, Orissa. He is also the President of the Governing Body of Orissa Christian Theological College and the Executive Committee Member of the United Evangelical Lutheran Church in India. He is a man of Prayer and great commitment for the cause of people's liberation from bondage.

Bro. K. J. Markose is a member of Brothers of St Gabriel (Montfort Brothers). He is a lawyer and also has a postgraduate in history. He has been at the service of the poorest for about 30 years. He is an educationist, social worker, activist and lawyer. He works among the tribals of Santhals and Mundas of Jharkhand, and among the Dalits of Jharkhand and Orissa. Presently he is heavily engaged with the persecuted Christians of Kandhamal, in rebuilding the society and trying to instill courage among them to claim their rights back.

Rt. Rev. Dr. Samson Das is the Bishop of Diocese of Cuttack, Church of North India. As a dynamic leader he shoulders many important responsibilities, He is currently the Moderator of Episcopal Commissary, Diocese of Chhatishgarh, CNI; Chairman of Utkal Christian Council, Orissa; Chairman of Utkal Christian Literature Board; Chairman of Stewart Schools & College; Chairman  of Orissa Christian Theological College, Gopalpur on Sea, Orissa; Chairman of Christian Hospital, Berhampur, Orissa and Chairman of the Bible Society of India, Orissa Auxiliary.

Mr. Vijay K. Swain is currently Project In-charge of Orissa Chapter at SPAR, which is working with poor and marginalized people through participatory approach. He is engaged in capacity building of the rural poor through formation and strengthening of People's Organization. The great responsibility of the organization fell on his  shoulders. From that very moment he spiritualized all his activities by his presence, counsel and wise leadership. His cheerful personality, exemplary conduct and extraordinary traits instantly gets him a distinct place in the hearts of all people with whom he comes into contact with. He is a person who believes in bringing about change for the better through hard work and a team work crossing many boundaries.

Mr. Kasta Dip belongs to the Church of North India. As a young and committed person he holds an important role in the Church of North India as

Coordinator – Justice, Peace & Reconciliation (Dalit & Tribal Concerns) from 2009 till date. He served as Youth Coordinator of CNI from 2004 to 2009. He is also serving as the Coordinator of South Asia Christian Youth Network. He is a Post Graduate in English Literature and hails from a Dalit community from Western Orissa district of Balangir.

Mr. Dibin Samuel works as a senior newsperson in Christian Today, a leading Christian news publication. He also contributes articles on religion and spirituality to numerous magazines and websites across the country. Currently, he is part of the Washington-based Christian Post, a pan-denominational newspaper presenting events affecting and involving Christian leaders, church bodies and mission agencies. Having covered a wide range of issues in the South Asian region including the HIV/AIDS epidemic, Dibin presently sheds light on issues relating to domestic violence, minorities and other often underserved populations. Dibin maintains a strong, persistent stand for Christ and biblical truths.

Ms. Elizabeth Joy is a Participant in God's Mission presently through Meora World Mission (Inclusive Communities in Mission Network), one of the initiatives of Jyothi Enterprises, which she heads as the Director. She served the Council for World Mission (CWM) as Executive Secretary for Mission Education from October 2002-January 2011. Currently she is pursuing her PhD at King's College London. She has also served the Student Christian Movement of India as the first Woman General Secretary prior to joining CWM. She is an activist, an inspiring leader and a Missionary who has travelled far and wide to bear witness to Christ's love for all.

Rev. S.S Majaw is an ordained presbyter of the Presbyterian Church of India, Khasi Jaintia Presbyterian Synod Sepngi. He was born on 14 April 1959. Presently he is the Administrative Secretary, General Assembly Presbyterian Church of India i/c Christian Communication, Theological Education, Presbyterian Women's Fellowship, i/c  Partner Churches and Councils: World Communion of Reformed Churches (WCRC), World Association Christian Communication (WACC), Presbyterian Church of USA, Presbyterian Church of Netherlands, National Council of Churches in India.

Fr. Ajay Kumar Singh is the head of Social Wing of Catholic Archdiocese of Cuttack-Bhubaneswar, Orissa. He presently coordinates the relief and rehabilitation efforts in Kandhamal on behalf of Catholic Church. He has been in social action since 2001. He hails from Kandhamal district and works with deep commitment and zeal facing much  hardship and trials in the contexts of his work and witness. He is a person who is very innovative and dreams with hope for a revolutionary change where the world all over beginning with his local troubled Kandhamal contexts will experience peace with justice.

Ms. Gwyneth Morus Jones hails from Wales, in the UK and Welsh is her first language. She is married and a mother of two children and three grandchildren. She is a retired school teacher. With her capacity as a retired teacher she is presently a member of a Welsh Assembly Government appointed body which promotes the Welsh language. Gwyneth is a member of the Union of  Welsh Independents (UWI), a congregational church and a Chairperson of the UWI since 2005. She represents the UWI on the Churches Dalit Support Group. She is a member of the CWM Trustee Body since 2006.

She had held the national chair of a number of voluntary movements in Wales.

Rev. Zosangliana Colney is an ordained minister of the Presbyterian Church of India, Mizoram Synod. He is the Executive Secretary of the Mizoram Synod. He shoulders many responsibilities as the Chairman of various committees under the Mizoram Synod such as Mizo Sunday School Union, Mizoram Synod Hospital, Education, Music, Synod Property, Women Department, Research and Evaluation Wing. He was the Secretary of the Mission Board, Mizoram Synod for two terms during the year 2001-2006. He is also Secretary (Jr.) Presbyterian Church of India General Assembly. Presently he is the Chairperson of the Indian Mission Association, Council Member of the Christian Medical College, Vellore, Tamil Nadu and member of the American Association of Missiology. He is a dynamic preacher, church leader and he is well known for his Bible Studies.

Dr. John Dayal is a member of the National Integration Council, Government of India for a second term now which is chaired by the Prime Minister of India. He is a journalist by profession and occasional documentary filmmaker. He has been a human rights activist as a student and journalist since the late Sixties. His book on the Indian Emergency (1975-77) is a major document of that period. He edited the monumental Gujarat 2002 – Untold and Retold Stories, on the anti-Muslim genocide in the state of Gujarat. His latest book is "A Matter of Equity –Interrogating Indian Secularism" published in 2007. The next book is on Kandhamal - Orissa. He was the National President, All India Catholic Union (2004-2008 - Founded in 1919) also Founder Secretary General, All India Christian Council (1999). John was National President of the All India Catholic Union, the country's main Catholic Laity movement, an internationally respected and honoured Journalist and Human Rights and Peace activist. He has spent years developing his database on peace and human rights issues, particularly right wing violence against Christians in India. He is married to Mercy Mariamma. They have a daughter, Karuna, a Journalist, and a son Jason. John continues his research into Hindutva and its interface with Christianity in contemporary India.

Mr. Jonathan Leckler is from the Church of South India, Diocese of Madras. During the brief period from August 2010 untill May 2011 he was an Intern with the National Council of Churches in India. He hails from a Pastor's Family. He did his Masters in Social work and also completed his Bachelors in Theology He is deeply interested in Dalit issues and Theology. His strength lies in his commitment for the cause of Justice to the communities at the margins, willingness to learn and ability to make friends.

Dr. Kaushalya **(Kaushal Panwar)** hails from Haryana state. She has done her Ph.D from JNU, New Delhi and presently serves as Assistant Professor, Dept of Sanskrit Motilal Nehru College, University of Delhi & Executive Member of Dalit Writers Association. Being born and brought up in the midst of caste violence in the society, her experience in life is the greatest lesson and the most powerful instrument that shaped her for what she is today. She is an ardent learner, teacher and prolific writer. Her involement in empowerment of women and the socially austracized group is clearly seen in her active participation in various seminars and consultations across the country. To her credit she has written 3 books *Sanhitaon Main Shudra, Praachin Bhartiye Samaj Main Shudra Avem Stri, Dharmshaastriya Shudra Vishayak Avadharana* and many of her articles are widely read and published in renowned magazines and various research journals. She is a much sought after Dalit scholar today and an activist.

Rev. Nathanial BM is a Deacon working in the Diocese of Amritsar serving at the Christ Church Cathedral, Amritsar. He is a graduate from the United Bible Seminary, Pune with a Bachelor of Divinity. He also serves in the Department of Communication Center of the Diocese. He is a young and committed servant of God for the downtrodden people of tribal and dalit in the society. The commitment to serve people and the society is the source of his strength.

Prof. Mammen Varkey is the Editor-in-Chief of the fortnightly People's Reporter and the Director of the ecumenical collective, Vichara, of academics and activists. He is deeply engaged in studies and research on economic, socio-political and theological topics and issues. He is a former member of the Syndicate of the University of Kerala and former Principal of Bishop Moore College, Mavelikara.

Rev. Laldawngliana is an ordained presbyter from Presbyterian Church of India, Manipur Synod. He was the Administrative Secretary General Assembly of the Presbyterian Church of India between 2002-2010. Presently stationed at Imphal, Manipur. He was also the Secretary for Council for World Mission – South Asia Regional Council for a period of 2007-2010. His deep commitment to his pastoral ministry is the source of his strength and blessings for all those who work with him. He is married and blessed with two sons and one daughter.

Rev. Dr. Roger Gaikwad comes from a strong spiritual heritage and academic excellence. He has given leadership, to the Church, theology fraternity and the ecumenical movement at different levels. His latest assignment before joining NCCI as General Secretary was as the Principal of Aizawl Theological College in Mizoram. He was also formerly the Director of SCEPTRE (a non-residential theological training programme), Senate of Serampore College (University) during June 2002 – January 2008.

Mrs. Rosnara Mohanty has been working in the field of social work since last 17 years mostly in the remote areas of Kalahandi and Kandhamal district of Orissa. She has a rich experience in working on the issues related to the survival of human beings like Right to land, work, and food. She is also actively involved in issues such as health, education, livelihood development etc. As a social activist she believes in the importance of strengthening and capacity building of grass root level CBOs, leadership development of rural youths. In recent years she was intensely involved in peace building activities.

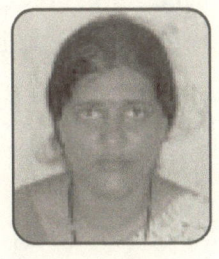

Mr. Samuel Philip Mathew is a Research Scholar in the History Department at Jamia Millia Islamia in Delhi. Specializing in Medieval Indian History, he is working on the 16th and 17th Centuries. Sam is a member of the NCCI Commission on Tribals. He is also one of the representatives from NCCI in the Joint Working Committee of National United Christian Forum. He belongs to the Mar Thoma Church and is youth secretary for the Delhi Diocese. A young ecumenist, he is also the spokesperson of a Delhi based ecumenical youth network called Delhi Christian Youth Forum. As an activist on socio political fronts, he was engaged with WSF in the past and is closely associated with student's movements. 'Faith and Politics' is a topic on which he interacts with young people across the country regularly.

Mr. Vanlalruatkima is an active and vibrant youth leader. He hails from Haflong Cachar Hill Tribe, Assam. Presently he has in his cap several important responsibilities at his local church as Committee member in the youth department and Adult Sunday School teacher. He is also Secretary of the Presbyterian Youth Fellowship of India General Assembly, Committee member in the PYF, Cachar Hill Tribe Synod and Asst. Leader of Haflong District Youth Fellowship. His strength lies on his commitment towards serving God and serving others without any reservations.

Ms. Sunita Tandi has been working in the field of social work since last 8 year mostly in the remote areas of Kalahandi and Kondhamal district, Orissa. Her experience includes community health management, sustainable agricultural development and working on land and forest right. A sincere and committed social worker, she is presently involved in peace building activities.

Prof. T. Vanlaltlani hails from a small village in eastern side of Mizoram. She started her Theological education from Bachelor of Theology course in Aizawl Theological College, Bachelor of Divinity in Serampore, Master of Theolgy in United Theological College, Doctor of Theology in SATHRI. She started her teaching ministry in Aizawl Theological College in 1983. After getting D.Th degree in Religions she was promoted to the rank of Associate Professor and continued to climb the ladder to the rank of Professor since Nov.1, 2008. She authored two books in English and five books in Mizo and additionally has written over 100 Articles both in English and Mizo. She is married to Mr. P.B. Khawla and is blessed with two sons Isaac and Gideon. Being a feminist theologian and activist, she is actively involved in political empowerment of women in Mizoram state in various ways as resource persons, as participants and as organizers. Her commitment to the Church and to the theological education makes her to be what she is today.

Rev. Dr. Chilkuri Vasantha Rao is an ordained minister of Medak Diocese, Church of South India. He teaches Old Testament at the Andhra Christian Theological College, Hyderabad. He has done his Doctoral Studies at the University of Hamburg, Germany and has been a Senior Visiting Scholar at the Harvard University Divinity School, USA. He has published several books on Ecology and Indigenization. He is presently the Principal of the Andhra Christian Theological College and adviser to the Student Christian Movement of India, Andhra Pradesh Region. To his credit he has several books and many articles published.

Rev. Vincent Rajkumar is a Presbyter of the Church of South India belongs to Karnataka Diocese, Bangalore. Presently serves as Director of Christian Institute for Study of Religion and Society (CISRS). A good orator and preacher and down to earth servant of God.

Dr. Hrangthan Chhungi hails from the Presbyterian Church of India, Mizoram Synod. She earned her Doctorate degree in the field of Old Testament. Currently serving as an Executive Secretary, Commission on Tribal and Adivasi, National Council of Churches in India. She is an ecumenist and activist with a theology of liberation working for the socially ostracized and oppressed communities. She has many articles published to her credit. Formerly Chhungi was the Dean for the North East Region, TAFTEE, Bangalore (2004-2006) and also Dean, Indian School of Ecumenical Theology, Ecumenical Christian Centre, Bangalore (2006-2008). She is actively engaged in biblical interpretation through the eyes of the tribal community, women and the nature around us.

Rev. Lalramliana Pachuau is an ordained minister of the Presbyterian Church of India, Mizoram Synod. Currently he is the Administrative Senior, Presbyterian Church of India General Assembly, stationed in Shillong. He is the Chairperson of the Commission on Tribal and Adivasi of the National Council of Churches in India. Rev Pachuau has deep concern towards the oppressive social structure in India that hierarchically subdued women, tribal and dalits in the society. He is known for his preaching eloquence among the Youth.

Rev. Dr. Vanlalchhuanawma is the Principal of Aizawl Theological College in Mizoram. Prior to this, he was a Lecturer, Registrar and Vice Principal of the same college. As a matter of fact, he was also the Founder Secretary of the Mizo Theological Association. For many years, Rev. Vanlalchhuanawma has been involved in Tribal-Dalit Interface and has contributed to ecumenism through Northeast India Christian Council as Convener of Church Union since 2000 till 2009. He did his B.A. (Distn.) - St. Edmund's College, Shillong, BD at Union Biblical Seminary, Yavatmal, and M.Th at Union Theological College, D.Th. - SATHRI, Bangalore.

Dr.H.T Sangliana, born on 1st June 1942 in Mizoram, joined the elite Indian Police Service in 1967 and was allotted the Karnataka cadre. He held various posts in his illustrious and impressive career in the India Police Service.

He was the Commissioner of Police of Bangalore city and retired as Director General of Police. During his service as a police officer, he had an impressive record. Movies "SP Sangliana" (Part I,II,III) have been made in the regional language Kanada and are based on his true life experiences.

After retiring, he ran for the seat of Lok Sabha and was a member of the 14th Lok Sabha of India and represented the Bangalore North constituency of Karnataka from of the Bharatiya Janata Party (BJP). He was expelled for voting in favour of the United Progressive Alliance (UPA) Government in the confidence motion in Lok Sabha on July 22, 2008.

Mr. H.T Sangliana has been awarded 3 Doctorate Degrees for his immense hardwork and service for the people of India.

Bishop A.S.Hemrom earned his Mater of Theology from Gurukul Theological College, Chennai. Presently he is an Executive Director, Human Resource Development Centre, GEL Church(an official organ of the church which promote and implements developmental activities in church and society), a Visiting Professor, Gossner Theological College, Ranchi (teaching theology & Adivasi  theology), Chairperson, Adivasi Desk, UELCI. He had published a few Articles presented on socio-theological issues published in books & journals at national and international publications.

Ms. Masophy Kengoo hails from the state of Manipur belongs to the Tangkhul Naga tribe. She did her Bachelor of Divinity from the John Roberts Theological Seminary Shillong. She is presently working with the Student Christian Movement of India as the Study Secretary for Women's Desk.

"Dalit – Tribal Interface:
Healing and Restoration"

Programme Schedule

"Dalit – Tribal Interface: Healing and Restoration"

(From Causes and Aftermath of the Kandhamal Violence 2007/2008 towards Peace, Justice and Reconciliation)

January 17-22, 2011, The Crown Hotel, Bhubaneswhar, Orissa

Organized by the Council for World Mission in partnership with National Council of Churches in India –Commission on Tribal and Adivasi and Presbyterian Church of India

---

Arrival - 17-01-2010: Departure – 22-01-2010

DAY 1 – 17/01/2011 (Monday)

6:00 pm – 6:30 pm: A Core-Group Committee Meeting at Princess Hall

6:30 pm – 7:30 pm: An informal meeting of the Delegates; a time to know more about each other at Princess Hall

Announcement and Information

DAY 2 – 18/01/2011 (Tuesday)

7:30 am – 8:30 am: Breakfast

INAUGURAL FUNCTION AT KINGS'S COURT

9:00 am – 9:30 am: **Welcome Speech**:

Bishop Samson Das, Bishop of Cuttack Diocese, CNI and

Dr. Hrangthan Chhungi, Executive Secretary, NCCI-COT

Opening Address:
Ms. Elizabeth Joy, Executive Secretary, Mission Education, CWM

Lighting of the Lamp:

9:30 am – 10:15 am: **Worship and Bible Study:**

Worship Leader: Ms.Ennah Nsofu, CWM

Bible Study: Bishop Yuhanon Mor Meletius, Malankara Orthodox Syrian Church

10:15 am – 10:30 am: **Inaugural Speech:**

Bishop Subas Chandra Gouda (JELC), President, Utkal Christian Council, Orissa

10:30 am – 11:00 **Greetings:**

Rev. Lalramliana Pachuau, Senior Administrative, PCI (Chairperson Commission on Tribal and Adivasi – NCCI)

Rev. Dr. Roger Gaikwad, General Secretary, NCCI

Ms. Ibatista Shylla, Progamme Secretary, YWCA

11:00 am – 11:20 am: **Tea Break**

11:20 am – 12:15 pm: **Keynote Address and Discussion:** Dr. Kaushal Panwar, Assistant Professor at Delhi University on **"Healing and Restoration towards Peace,**

Justice and Reconciliation of the Dalit and Tribal Communities in India".

Moderator: Dr. John Dayal, Member, National Integration Council, Government of India

12:15 pm – 1:00 pm:	**Case Presentation by** Fr. John Thundiyl, and Mr. Prafulla Samatara
	Moderator – Ms. Barbara Dohling
1:00 pm – 2:30 pm:	**Lunch Break**
2:30 pm – 4:00 pm:	**Panel Discussion** on "Legal Battle: Pinning Down the Perpetrators to Move Forward Promoting Peace, Justice and Reconciliation"
	Panellists are: Adv. B.D. Das, Bro. Markose and Adv. Kranti LC
	Moderator: Ms. Anjna Masih
4:00 pm – 4: 20 pm;	Tea/Coffee Break
4:20 pm – 5:20 pm:	**Panel Discussion** on "Causes of the Kandhamal Violence 2007/2008"
	Panellists are Mr. Aksheya Kumar, Dr. John Dayal, Fr. Ajoy Singh
	Moderator: Mr. Angelious Michael
5:20 pm – 6: 40 pm:	**Church's Response for "Healing and Restoration Towards, Peace, Justice and Reconciliation for Dalits and Tribals Communities"**
	Panellists are: Bishop Samson Das, Rev. Dr. Roger Gaikwad, Rev. Laldawngliana
	Moderator: Dr. (Mrs) S. Manohar Rao
6:40 pm – 7:00 pm:	**Feed Back of Day 2:**
	Moderator: Rev. Dr. Ch. Vasantha Rao
7:30 pm – 8:30 pm:	Dinner

DAY 3: 19-01-2011 (Wednesday)

7:30 am – 8:30 am: **Breakfast**

9:00 am – 9:45 am: **Devotion**

                        Leader: Rev. Nancy, CWM

                        Bible Study: Rev. Zosangliana Colney

9:45 am – 11:00 am   **Panel Discussion** on "Healing and Restoration Towards Peace, Justice and Reconciliation of the Dalit and Tribal Communities in India – Role of Christian Organizations and Theological Education"

                        Panellists are – Rev. Vincent Rajkumar, Rev. Dr. Vanlalchhuanawma, and Bishop A.S. Hemrom, Dr. T. Vanlaltlani

                        Moderator: Mr. Kasta Dip

11:00 am -11:20 am: **Tea/Coffee break**

11:20 am – 12:00 pm: **Presentations** on "Convergences and Mutual Learning"

                        Rev. Raj Bharath Patta (from Dalit perspective) and Dr. Hrangthan Chhungi (tribal Perspective)

                        Moderator: Mr. Samuel Philip Mathew

12:00 pm – 1:00 pm: Group Discussion

1:00 pm – 2:30 pm: **Lunch Break**

2:30 pm – 3:30 pm: **Panel Discussion on** "Roles of Christian Media as Channel of Healing and Restoration towards Peace, Justice and Reconciliation for Dalit and Tribal Communities in India"

                        Panellists are: Prof. Mammen Varkey (Chief Editor People's Report), Mr. Anto Kara (ENI Correspondent), Mr. Dibin Samuel (Senior News Person, Christian Today), women....??

Moderator: Mr. Edwin Daniel

3:30 pm – 4:00 pm;   **Buzz Group**

4:00 pm – 4:20 pm: **Tea/Coffee Break**

At Ruby Hall

4:20 pm – 5:20 pm: **Group Presentation** on "Dalit and Tribal Women - Instruments of Peace and Reconciliation amidst Violence"

Presenters: Mr. Angelious Michael, Ms.Rosnara and Ms. Masophi Kengoo

Moderator: Adv. Brother Markose

5:20 pm – 6:20 pm   **Church's Response on** "Healing and Restoration Towards, Peace, Justice and Reconciliation for Dalits and Tribals Communities"

Panellists are: Rev. Nathanial B.M., Bishop Bijay Kumar Nayak, Bishop Yuhanon Mor Meletius, Rev. Nancy

Moderator: Ms. Ibatista Shylla

6:20 pm – 7:00 pm: **Feedback of Day 3: Leader** – Mr. Vijay Kumar Swain

7:30 pm – 8:30 pm: Dinner

DAY 4 – 20-01-2011 (Thursday)
AN EXPOSURE TRIP TO KANDHAMAL (Provisions such as Bags of Rice, Bags of Dhal, bags of Potatoes, Bags of Cooking Oil, Basic Medicines for CNI hospital will be taken along from Bhubaneshwar to be distributed among the people of Kandhamal)

4:30 am: Leaving to Kandhamal from the Crown

9:00 am – 10:00 am: Break Fast at Diocesan Office, CNI Bishop's

House, (BF be packed or organized by us)

Host: Bishop Vijay Kumar Nayak

10:00 am – 1:00 pm: Visit to near by Villages

1:00 pm – 2:00 pm: Lunch Break at Bishop's Residence

2:00 pm – 5:00 pm: Face to Face Conversation with the Victims of Kandhamal Riot 2007/2008

Listening to their stories; and a time to interact with them.

(Bishop will invite people from different villages of the Dalit and Tribal Communities from all faiths. An interface of the dalit and tribal communities will be the first of its kind after the Kandhamal violence 2007/2008)

4:45 pm – 5:00 pm: Tea

5:00 pm – 10:00 pm: Journey Back to Crown, Bhubaneshwar from Kandhamal

DAY 5 – 21-01-2011 (Friday)

8:30 am - 9:30 am: **Break Fast**

10:00 am – 10:45 am: **Devotion**

Leader: Ms. Gwyneth Morus Jones, CWM

Bible Study: Rev. Dr. Ch. Vasantha Rao

10:45 am – 11:30 am: **Speech on "Kandhamal Riot: Response from the Government for Healing and Restoration" by Dr. H.T. Sangliana** Vice-Chairperson, Commission on Minorities, Govt. of India, New Delhi

11:30 am – 12:00 am: **Tea/Coffee Break**

12:00 am – 1:00 pm: **Critical Analysis of the Conflicts between Dalits & Tribals,** by Mr. Edwin Daniel & Rev. Raj Bharath Patta

1:00 pm – 2:30 pm:	**Lunch Break**
2:30 pm – 3:15pm:	**Group Discussion**
3:15 pm – 4:00 pm	**Group Reports and Plenary:** Leader Ms. Elizabeth Joy and Rt.Rev. Bishop B.S.Devamani
4:00 pm – 4:45 pm:	**Statement and Action Plan Presentation:**
	Moderator: Rev. Dr. Ch. Vasantha Rao
4:45 pm – 5:15 pm	**Tea/Coffee Break**
5:15 pm - 6:00 pm:	**Closing Function**
	Leader: Rev. Lalramliana Pachuau
	Bible Reading and Prayer: Rev. T.J. John
	Felicitation by Rev. Laldawngliana
	Responses:
	Vote of Thanks: Dr. Hrangthan Chhungi
	Prayer and Benediction: Rev. Raj Bharath Patta
6:00 pm – 7:30 pm:	Cultural Evening: The Orissa State Cultural Troupe
7:30 pm – 8:30 pm:	Dinner
8:30 pm – 10:00 pm:	Farewell Party for all the participants

DAY 6 – 22-01-2011 (Saturday)

Departure from the Crown: Last check out by 12:00 noon.

Note: Dr. HT Sangliana, Vice-Chairperson, Commission on Minorities, Central Government of India, Delhi also will be with us on the final day.

For Kandhamal Visit permission needs to be taken from The Ministry of Home Department, the Orissa Government from Bhubaneshwar. Mr. Vijay Kumar will take care of that on 18ᵗʰ. Names of all the delegates who will be visiting Kandhamal needs to be given to the Home Ministry Department. This is just to be on the safe side for security concerns by the state authority.

Statement and Action Plan Committee members

Leader- Rev. Dr. Ch. Vasantha Rao

Members: Mr. Edwin Daniel, Ms. Ibatista Shaila, Bishop. A.S. Hemrom, Mr. Kasta Dip, Mr. Samuel Philip Mathew, Prof. Mammen Varkey, Rev. Raj Bharath Patta, Dr. Hrangthan Chhungi, Ms. Elizabeth Joy

(first meeting of the committee will be on the 19th evening after Dinner)

www.ingramcontent.com/pod-product-compliance
Lightning Source LLC
Chambersburg PA
CBHW060357030726
47497CB00003B/743